USA TODAY BESTSELLING AUTHOR
NANCY WARREN

CRUMBS AND MISDEMEANORS

THE GREAT WITCHES BAKING SHOW
BOOK 6

Crumbs and Misdemeanors, The Great Witches Baking Show, book 6

Copyright © 2021 by Nancy Warren

ISBN: ebook 978-1-990210-04-4

ISBN: print 978-1-990210-03-7

Cover Design by Lou Harper of Cover Affairs

Ambleside Publishing

INTRODUCTION

Bread is supposed to be the staff of life—not a murder weapon.

Every baker has their weak spot. For Poppy it's bread. So, when The Great British Baking Contest hits bread week, she's as fragile as an overbaked croissant. Just when she needs to keep all her focus on flour, water, yeast and salt, another ingredient enters the mix. Death.

Someone is not who they appear to be, and secrets from the past are bringing deadly consequences to the present. Poppy isn't only a contestant in the long-running TV show, she's also a witch and reluctant amateur sleuth. With the rest of her coven, assorted animal helpers and her ghostly sidekick Gerry, Poppy needs to solve the murder before someone else dies.

~

If you haven't met Rafe Crosyer yet, he's the gorgeous, sexy vampire in *The Vampire Knitting Club* series. You can get his origin story free when you join Nancy's no-spam newsletter at NancyWarrenAuthor.com.

Come join Nancy in her private Facebook group where we talk about books, knitting, pets and life. www.facebook.com/groups/NancyWarrenKnitwits

CRUMBS AND MISDEMEANORS

CHAPTER 1

*B*read had never been my jam, so to speak. Every baker will tell you that there is one type of bake they struggle with—it might be patisserie, biscuits, or getting a fluffy and light genoise. For me, it was bread. I don't know why I had such a tough time with that seemingly oh so simple staple. It eluded me. Was I being punished by the gluten gods for having a wickedly sweet tooth? The closer we got to bread week, the more my bread wouldn't perform. Either it didn't rise properly, or it was too dry, too wet, too heavy, or the crust was hard.

I practiced and practiced—everything from caraway seed loaf to sourdough, although I was pretty sure that the judges wouldn't demand a sourdough loaf, as it took too long. But still, I wanted to cover all my bases, leave no pizza stone unturned. I couldn't stop my mind from racing. We were in week six of *The Great British Baking Contest,* and the competition was getting fierce. I needed to be prepared to defend my weakest spot, my Achilles' heel of baking. And so I kept up the bread-making. Day after boring day.

As much as I despaired, so too did Mildred, my kitchen ghost. Now I was used to Mildred being a bit of a Debbie downer; she was always griping at me for taking the easy way out, using "fancy technology" to whisk or whip or not knowing the "basics," which in her Victorian opinion were plum duff (which didn't, incidentally, have any plums, just suet, dried fruit and egg) or bread made with hop yeast. "Ye begin with hops boiled in water and some potatoes boiled and bruised," she instructed me. Like I didn't have enough recipes to try.

Even Gina, my best friend, refused to come over and do another taste test. "Pops, I don't want to come over and sample rye rusks. Really, love, you're going off the deep end." I felt for her. No doubt she couldn't eat any more combinations of flour, yeast, salt and water plus whatever other ingredients I could dream up. Bread either rises and has good texture and flavor or it doesn't. It's not like cake, where you can hide a multitude of faults under icing.

"Bread is boring," Gina said. "Do your best. You'll be fine."

It was easy for her to brush the crumbs under the carpet and say things would be fine. Gina wasn't a baker; she was a makeup and hair artist—and an excellent one at that. She might think bread was dull, but it was a foundation skill I was going to have to get right. Bread was unforgiving when you messed up, and I couldn't seem to do anything but make a mess.

By the end of the week, I had gone through sacks of flour, fresh yeast, dried yeast, and a sourdough starter I'd made myself weeks ago, and not one single perfect loaf emerged from my frantic efforts. One evening spent in her favorite spot in the kitchen left Gateau, my black cat familiar, looking like she'd been out in a snowstorm. After that, she watched me from an armchair in the living room. Even my own familiar was tired of my klutzy ways.

It wasn't only vanity propelling my desperate attempt at bread mastery. I was worried that if I didn't shine this week, then my days on *The Great British Baking Contest* would be numbered, and then so would my time at Broomewode Hall, *just* when I felt like I was making progress discovering more about my birth parents. I could feel in my gut that my dad was a local, someone from Broomewode Village born and bred, and this week I intended to act on this intuition. Which meant sticking around.

Which is why, by the time Thursday evening was approaching, I'd decided I was going to need some expert help on the bread front. And who better to ask than my coven sister Eve? I called her when I knew she'd be setting up for the dinner shift at the inn. After a nice natter catching up, I explained my predicament and was immediately soothed by Eve's calm manner and her gentle words of encouragement.

"I'm sure it's not that bad, Pops," she said. "You've come so far in the competition. Don't let a bout of nerves throw you off now."

I assured Eve it wasn't nerves. More like a case of bread-stick fingers—I couldn't knead dough properly to save my life.

Eve laughed. "Look, if that's really true, then why don't you come to the inn tomorrow morning? On Fridays, Eloise is in the kitchen. She's our pastry chef. She hasn't been here long, but her bread's excellent. I'll have a word with her later and see if she'll give you some tips."

I jumped up and down on the spot, irritating Gateau, who

was napping by my side. I thanked Eve, hung up, and went to face the dreaded mess in my kitchen.

⁓

"POPPY WILKINSON, REPORTING FOR BREAD DUTY," I said brightly, raising my arm in a salute, like an actor in *Dad's Army,* a show my adopted dad had always loved.

Behind the bar, Eve collapsed into giggles. "Don't worry. Eloise isn't that tough of a taskmaster." She paused. "Well, maybe she is a bit. A sweet girl but a little stern. She'll put you through your paces. But that's the idea, right?"

I laughed a little nervously and took a seat on a barstool, setting my small suitcase beside me. Gateau had scampered off the minute I opened the car door—no doubt anxious to get away from me and my current obsession.

"By the looks of you, a coffee wouldn't go amiss."

I nodded. My baking antics had truly worn me out this week, and the competition hadn't even started yet. I should have found time to rest, but I was so worried about my bread-making skills that I kept pushing myself all week. I watched with gratitude as Eve made me a cup of hot black coffee.

She talked about her week, and I listened to her chatter about the locals, who'd had a little too much to drink, whose nephew was moving to London, and (most interestingly) that Edward had been unofficially promoted to Broomewode gamekeeper.

"That's great news," I said. I liked Edward. He'd only recently been hired as a gardener, and now he was acting as the gamekeeper as well.

"Even better, he and Lauren were spotted on a date in the

next village over. A new French bistro," Eve said. "Very romantic."

"I'm glad," I said, and I meant it. Lauren had been through a terrible time, losing her fiancé on the day they should have married. From what I could sense, Edward was a good man.

I took a sip of coffee and let out a deep sigh. I was going to have to dig deep this weekend. And if that meant a little caffeine injection every few hours, then so be it.

"Ah, here's our new pastry chef now," Eve said, and I looked up to see a young woman approaching. She was tall, with a mane of fine hair caught into a butterfly clip and a smattering of freckles, which danced across the bridge of her nose. Her square glasses lent her a serious air, and she was wearing a crisp white apron. She looked to be similar in age to me, but she stooped a little, almost like she was embarrassed by her height and was trying to shrink herself.

"Eloise, meet Poppy, your student for the morning."

I grinned and stood up to shake Eloise's hand.

"I hear you've been doing battle with dough this week," she said, her voice deep and mellow.

"Battle is the word," I agreed. "Thank you so much for agreeing to show me a few tips. You've no idea what it means to me."

Eloise assured me she'd share her knowledge of how to work with different grains and textures. "Wheat, rye and barley—they're all different beasts. You can't treat them the same way," she warned.

I drained my coffee and then followed her through to the kitchen, which was behind a set of double doors adjacent to the bar.

"Good luck," Eve called out.

I'd never spent much time in the inn's kitchen before, and I was surprised by how large it was. In spite of the inn's antiquity, the kitchen was modern, home to huge stainless-steel gas ranges, multiple fridges and worktops. The place was gleaming, and the scent of lemon cleaner mingled with baked goods. At 9 a.m., the morning sun shone through the windows. As much as I loved my cottage, I couldn't wait to bake in such a well-equipped and spacious kitchen. I said as much to Eloise, but she just shrugged. "It's not that glamorous when you're elbow-deep in flour."

"We've got the kitchen to ourselves?" I was surprised and pleased not to have kitchen staff overlooking my sad efforts.

"Sol is outside unloading a delivery with his sous chef, so he'll be coming in and out. Don't mind him. He doesn't interfere with my work, and I stay out of his."

Sounded to me like Eloise and the head chef weren't best pals.

"Are you sure you have time to help me?" I didn't want to get under her feet or in her way at work.

"Sure. I've already finished the desserts for today. I've a bit of time. Happy to help. Come in the pantry and we'll collect our ingredients."

"Can I?" I half whispered, giddy with excitement. It wasn't a very rock-'n'-roll indulgence, but a big pantry with loads of shelving was a baker's catnip.

Eloise laughed. "Come on, then."

I slid back the heavy door and gasped in delight. It was wonderful. Rows and rows of tinned goods, marmalades and preserves; condiments of all kinds; oils and vinegars; a wall of spices, all neatly organized and labeled; mason jars containing cocoa, nuts and seeds. There were trays of pota-toes, onions and root vegetables; and giant sacks of flour, rice, and different sugars all grabbed my attention as I gazed about me.

"Wow," I said.

"Pretty special," Eloise said. "We try to use as much local produce as possible. Eve told me that you're a friend of Susan Bentley's—that's her honey over there. Her eggs are amazing, too. They have the perfect orange yolks."

I nodded in agreement. "Susan says they're happy eggs, as they come from happy hens. I think if I worked here, I'd spend all day in the pantry, sampling things and coming up with different recipes."

At that, Eloise frowned, and I felt like I'd touched a nerve. Maybe I was being too presumptuous. Working in a kitchen was a very different thing to being an amateur baker. It was a lot of hard work and long, unsociable hours.

"I wish," she replied. "Too busy folding a hundred crois-sants a day for that! Speaking of which."

She turned away from the pantry, pulled the doors to a close, and patted the work surface. Next to her hand was a huge steel mixing bowl, a set of electric scales and a wooden spoon. "I've worked in kitchens a long time," she said, "and if there's one thing I've learned in this business is that in order to stand out, you've got to come up with something that reflects who *you* are. Be the best, even if it's for one cake. Like the best turf cakes in York. Aim for making the local papers and becoming renowned for one thing."

I nodded eagerly, even though I had no idea what a turf cake was. I whipped a notebook out of my bag and flicked to a blank page. I wanted to remember every little detail.

"This is what I know about bread," she said, drawing herself up to her full height. "Yeast is a fickle mistress. You have to know how to handle her right; otherwise she'll spoil. And you have to let her do things in her own time. Most bread products usually have two separate occasions where they're left to rise. This'll be tricky for you tomorrow."

"They give us extra time for bread week," I said, nodding, "so that it can proof. The showstopper is filmed in two parts, even though it's cut to look like one long session."

I clapped my hand to my mouth. I so wasn't supposed to give away any show secrets.

Eloise laughed. "Don't worry. I won't tell."

She continued to share her bread tips, letting me know that after the first rise, I needed to punch all the gas out of the dough to get rid of any large bubbles that might have been created. "That way, the yeast stays strong enough for a second rise. This is how you get good texture," she said.

I already knew this, but it was theoretical knowledge, and for some reason, my brain and my hands didn't seem to be working together.

"Then the yeast will be strong enough for a second rise," she continued. "It's on this second rise that the bubbles will appear more even and create a better texture."

She continued, telling me that by the time I took my bread to the oven, I wanted "a medium firmness with uniform bubbles," she said. "If you leave it too long to rise, the yeast fizzles out."

"That's overproving, right?" I said, eager to display the little knowledge I *did* have.

She nodded. "If you want a light and airy texture, then those gas bubbles must stay intact. Breadmaking is more science than art. Your measurements must be exact. No throwing a little of this and a little of that in and thinking it'll work. In a cake batter, you often get away with sloppy measurements. Not with bread."

Were my troubles as simple as that? I was a little sloppy in my measurements. I began to feel better thinking that if I was careful to be precise this weekend, I might be all right.

"Right. I'm making a simple white French loaf for the morning. I only need two loaves. You can make it. Let's see how you do."

"Okay." I hoped I didn't fail my first test.

"I keep the white flour in here," she said, pulling out a metal-lined drawer that was her flour bin. We fetched yeast and salt from the pantry.

Next Eloise said she wanted to watch my technique. "Just be natural. Do your thing."

Yeah, like I could act naturally under the eye of a professional baker.

I started to weigh the flour, reminding myself that the world would be watching via their televisions whatever I did tomorrow, and in thinking of both those things managed to drop flour onto the counter, where it then spilled onto my jeans.

"I'd better fetch you an apron from the laundry delivery outside," Eloise said. Oh, I was off to a good start.

I picked up the sieve and carried on with the familiar routine but this time feeling more hopeful. I was so happy Eve had set up this quick teaching session with a bread baker who clearly knew her stuff.

I finished sieving and looked out of the open window, wondering whether to wait until Eloise returned. Seemed to be taking a long time to collect an apron. I caught sight of two men unloading crates of produce from a white van through the open window. One of the men was much bigger than the other, burly and tattooed, and he carried himself in such an assured manner that I was positive he was the head chef, Sol. The other man was much smaller and more wiry. He darted from the van to a loading trolley with quick, light steps. They seemed to be working in silence, in the kind of easy rhythm two people have when they've been working side by side for a long time.

Eloise emerged from the front of the van, apron in hand, and stopped by the chef. He put down a crate of potatoes with a look of sheer annoyance.

"I was hoping to catch you," Eloise said, her deep voice floating in through the open window.

"I'm busy," he replied. He had a gruff voice that suited his heavyset body.

"Just a quick word." She glanced at the other guy. "In private."

Sol looked at the other man and said something I couldn't quite catch.

The two of them moved away from the van and towards the window. I darted out of sight. I didn't want Eloise to think I was eavesdropping, although that was exactly what I was doing. Besides, if I moved, they might see me.

"If this is about money—" Sol said.

Eloise made a sound like a sigh or maybe a groan. "I only need a small advance. I—"

But Sol cut her off. "I can't keep giving you money. You've had advances on your last two paychecks, Eloise. It's too much. You get a good salary here. Why are you so hard up? Do you have some habit I should know about?"

"No. Nothing like that. I—lost all my savings. Things have been a bit tight. Just trying to get back on my feet."

There was a silence and I all but held my breath. Finally, Sol said, in a much gentler tone. "We all have our troubles."

I rose from my crouching position carefully and saw Sol shake his head. His hair caught the sun so that it glinted like the edge of a freshly polished steak knife.

Eloise turned, and I ducked again. If anyone was watching, I'd have looked like I was bobbing for apples. In June. Like a maniac.

I heard her clear her throat, and then her already deep voice lowered another notch. "Sol, I wouldn't ask if I didn't have to."

He scoffed. "Oh yeah? I'm surprised you *do* need the money after all you've been skimming off the top here."

There was a long silence. I felt my stomach contract. Wow. This was awkward. I'd only just met the poor girl, and now here I was, overhearing her money troubles. As a freelance graphic designer, I knew what it was like to find yourself in a tight spot when a client delayed payment or if there was too long a gap between jobs. You could work as hard as it was possible to work but still not make ends meet when the bills came rolling in. Poor Eloise. My heart went out to her.

The baker still hadn't replied.

"I didn't say anything when I found out because you're good at what you do," Sol said. "A bit moody, but you make the best croissants I've ever tasted, and you keep your head down at work. I like that. But ordering supplies and then fudging the invoices to look like they cost more than they did? That's some ballsy racket you've got going on. It's got to stop. Otherwise, I'll have to let you go."

"Oh, come on!" she shouted back. "What about the joints of meat I've seen you walking out with? You think I'm stupid?"

"You don't know what you're talking about." I saw him take a step toward her, looking furious. His hand fisted. I didn't pause to think. I pointed at the box of produce he'd placed on the ground. I said softly,

Crate.
Break.
Let your contents spill.
My wish fulfill.
As I will, so mote it be.

I barely got the first couple of words out when one side of the crate fell and potatoes rolled out.

"What the—" The chef rushed forward to rescue the rolling potatoes.

Eloise turned away. I dashed back to the prep area.

A moment later, she walked back into the kitchen, a big smile on her face, and handed me the apron. But even if I hadn't overheard that uncomfortable exchange, Eloise's smile wouldn't have distracted me from the worry in her eyes. She looked absolutely forlorn.

"No wonder you haven't had any success baking bread," she said, pointing at my mixing bowl, which so far only had flour in it. "You'd better get your skates on if you want to win bread week!"

CHAPTER 2

"*T*here you go, Pops," Florence said, gallantly setting a glass of red wine on the table. "You look like you need it."

Coffee in the day, wine in the evening—that sounded about right. I thanked Florence and took a deep drink. If I thought I'd been exhausted practicing my bread-making skills all week, it was nothing compared with what Eloise put me through today. Sweet as pie, until she suddenly wasn't, Eloise was a tough taskmaster. I spent all morning helping her prepare bread for the inn's restaurant, which was fully booked for the weekend. We covered sourdough, rye, soda bread and granary—the loaves which, until now, I'd happily gobbled down at breakfast without giving a second thought to who made them or where the ingredients came from.

My head was spinning with all the knowledge Eloise had tried to impart in the time we had together. Flour processes, kneading techniques, how to use the right yeast, balance the levels of salt and judge the amount of proving time needed. My fingers ached, my back ached, and my feet ached. And did I feel ready for filming? Nope. I felt like I'd finished a grueling weekend of baking on camera, and we hadn't started yet.

If anything, Eloise's expertise and instinctive knowledge around bread dough had only made me more aware of my shortcomings. I just hoped that this brain of mine had soaked up some of her knowledge and could use it when it was crunch time. An early night was in order. This was my last chance to get some rest. No doubt I'd be dreaming of bread rising all night.

Florence settled herself beside me. She was wearing a khaki jumpsuit that complemented the chestnut curls that hung loosely around her shoulders. The remaining bakers had checked into their rooms in the late afternoon, and we were gathered at our usual table, poring over the menu. The pub was busy, the sound of laughter and wineglasses clinking filled the air, and I tried hard to unclench the muscles in my stomach, roll back my shoulders and let myself relax. It was Friday night. I'd worked hard, and now it was time to switch off for a few hours.

Darius walked over to take our food orders. He'd obviously been out in the sun this week, and his olive skin glowed. His black hair had grown a little, too, and he'd brushed it away from his forehead in a debonair style reminiscent of forties Hollywood heartthrobs. He greeted Florence with a grin, and they exchanged a few words in Greek, Florence tossing her hair over her shoulder coquettishly.

Hamish raised his eyebrows, but I'd long stopped being shocked by Florence's compulsive flirting. She was who she was, and there wasn't any harm in a little cheeky grin or six, so why not let her be? When Darius had finished flashing his perfectly white teeth at Florence, he turned his attention to the rest of us, and I ordered a chicken parmigiana. I needed protein and a little cheesy goodness to fill the gnawing ache in my belly.

Maggie caught my eye across the table and asked about my week. I shook my head miserably. "Tough. How about yours? What's your signature bake tomorrow?"

"A sweet soda bread," Maggie said, smiling, "with toasted pecans and chocolate chips. My grandchildren love it. I've been their favorite relative this week."

"I'm sure you're their favorite every week," I replied. If I had to sketch a picture of a loving grandmother, I was sure it would look exactly like Maggie. With her soft white hair, kindly smile, and round glasses, which hung around her neck on a golden chain, she was the perfect good-natured grandparent. I loved the elegant twin sets she wore, always in pastel hues. Today, she had on a pair of understated mother-of-pearl earrings, and I complimented them.

"A gift from my son last Christmas," she said, glowing.

Darius returned with a basket of sliced warm baguette. I moaned and declined a piece. "As if I can even look at bread right now," I said, shaking my head. "It's officially my enemy."

"It's a very good idea for you to stay away from the carbs, Poppy," Florence agreed, glancing at my belly. I was shocked. Had I gained weight? Or had she misunderstood?

Gaurav laughed. "I can never eat too much bread. I love it."

"It's delicious, but it doesn't love me back," I said. "I definitely don't have the knack."

"That's how I feel about patisserie," Hamish said. "The

knack—that's exactly the right word. It's like my brain isn't wired to make petite, precise cakes. I'm not neat enough. I don't have that delicate touch you need to get all those details right."

"Patisserie is like a distant dream to me," I replied. "I can't even get a simple loaf to rise properly." My insecurity was getting the better of me. Why was no one else fazed by bread week?

"Nonsense, Poppy," Florence said. "You're a super baker—surely something as simple as bread can't elude you?"

I shrugged, embarrassed to admit that it had.

I directed the attention away from me and onto Gaurav, asking about his plans for tomorrow. He was making a savory soda bread with beetroot and caraway seeds.

"I discovered that using yogurt mixed with a spoonful of milk, rather than buttermilk, works really well in this combination. I roast the beetroots with a little honey glaze to sweeten them up, and that complements the caraway perfectly. The loaf is a lovely pink color."

I was impressed. After experimenting all week with flavor combinations, I'd decided that my best chance of success was to keep things simple and classic with an Irish soda bread recipe.

"I'm worried that it might be a bit boring," I confided to Gaurav, "but if I get it right, then the caramelized onions and cheddar will be warm, earthy and wholesome."

He nodded. "Nothing wrong with sticking to a classic, especially if you don't feel like bread is your strong suit."

But as I listened to the others talk about their signature bake, I realized I was the only one playing it safe. Florence was making a lemon and black pepper loaf, which sounded incredible; Hamish a bacon and rosemary combination, which sounded lovely. No one seemed even remotely as nervous as me, which, of course, only heightened my nerves even further.

Luckily, all talk of bread ceased as our main courses arrived, and the table went silent for a moment, feasting on that first sumptuous bite of their chosen dish. As usual, I was ravenous, and the parmigiana was the perfect antidote to a day's hard work. I took another sip of red wine and listened to Florence gossip about a date she'd been on in the week. I'd no idea how she found the time for romance. Or Gaurav, either. Had everyone had a dose of some confidence potion this week? Wasn't I supposed to be the one with the potions?

It was only after I'd scraped every last morsel from my plate that I noticed Eve had left her usual position behind the bar. She was sitting at a table in the corner, hunched over what looked to be a deck of cards.

Florence followed my gaze. "Tarot!" she squealed. "I didn't know that Eve read tarot cards."

"Neither did I!" I said, equally surprised. Eve had kept that talent quiet.

"Let's go get a reading," Florence said, pulling on the sleeve of my cardigan.

"I don't think I want to know what's in my future," I said, trying to keep my voice light, but I meant it. I had enough visions of my own to contend with.

But Florence, being Florence, wouldn't take no for an answer. She dragged me over to Eve's table and, with a charming smile, asked if we could join her.

Eve obliged and pulled out two chairs. She said Darius had begged her for a quick reading after she'd revealed she read tarot. "It's a family tradition," she said, smiling, a playful look flitting across her face. "Have you ever had your cards read?"

I shook my head. The world of tarot cards was one I knew very little about apart from what I'd seen in the movies, which was mostly images of swirling incense, candles, beaded curtains, glass ceramics and death cards. I'd thought of tarot readers as mysterious and elaborately dressed—not my lovely down-to-earth Eve.

"Me first," Florence called out. "I'm wanting to know what —or who—is in my stars."

"Och, me too." I turned to see that Hamish, Gaurav, and Darius had joined us.

"You've drawn quite a crowd," I said to Eve.

She laughed and agreed to do one or two cards for everyone. "But not a full reading. We've still got work to do, Darius! This pub won't run by itself." Darius chuckled and agreed they'd get back to it in five minutes.

The others pulled up a stool, and Eve began to shuffle the cards. The cards were larger than I imagined a tarot deck to be and were obviously well-loved, as some of the edges were bent and beaten up. I suddenly felt nervous, although I couldn't think why.

Don't let the week get to you, Pops, I admonished myself. *You need to keep something in the tank for the weekend.*

Eve glanced around at her rapt audience. "You must think of a question that you'd like to ask the cards—just one, and then I'll pull one card from the deck."

Florence, ever dramatic, let her eyes flutter and took a deep breath in.

"Now remember that the cards are a practical guide to

help you create your own future," Eve said, lowering her voice. "You are in control. The cards work with whatever energy you bring, and whatever your current circumstances, the future can always be changed. Tarot is about intuition, learning to listen."

"Got it," Florence said with a grin.

"Are you asking if a tall, dark, handsome man will walk into your life? Because I can answer that one for free," Darius joked.

The glance she sent him in return should have come with a heat warning. Yeesh. Could someone get those two a room?

Luckily, Eve ignored Darius and turned over a card.

Florence glowed. "The Magician."

I studied the image, trying to figure out what it meant. The card was mustard yellow, a man in a white and red robe center stage, holding a scepter. On a table beside him was a gold goblet and some other items I couldn't quite make out. It looked more mysterious than magical.

"What does it mean?" Hamish asked.

"The card has many meanings, but here I feel it is about manifesting your destiny," Eve replied, her voice suddenly solemn. "Talent and power are at your fingertips if you put them to good use. You must keep your focus. It's best to keep your imagination open with this card—that way, you let the magic in."

Florence didn't say what she'd asked the card, but I guessed it was to do with her being a famous actress. The Magician must have been music to her ears. She smiled broadly, and Darius patted her gently on the shoulder.

"Gaurav, what about you?" Eve asked.

Florence switched seats, and Gaurav sat opposite Eve. He

looked nervous, but Eve reassured him that nothing bad would come from the cards. As with Florence, she instructed Gaurav to think of a question he wanted to ask the cards. He smiled. She drew a card.

"Oooh, you got The Lovers!" Florence squealed.

Poor Gaurav blushed beetroot.

"This card indicates a relationship coming into your life," Eve said. "It might be romantic in nature, but not necessarily—it could be any relationship where good communication is involved. This card can also indicate a choice, and it's here to remind you to follow your heart but not without examining honestly which path is best for you to follow."

Hamish nudged me and whispered, "That's got to be about him and the bridesmaid, right? Sounds like a proper romance."

"You're as bad as Florence," I chided playfully. "And Lauren was the bride-to-be."

"I heard that!" Florence said. "Time for you to face the cards, Poppy. I can't wait to see what you get."

I felt bad for implying that Florence was dramatic as I, too, closed my eyes and took a deep breath in. I was suddenly nervous. I thought I didn't want to know the future, but as soon as I let myself relax the question came to me.

"Done," I said to Eve solemnly.

She turned over the card.

"That does not look good," I said in a quiet voice. The card displayed a skeleton with a scythe.

"The DEATH card!" Florence shrieked.

"Now, now, calm down," Eve chided. "The death card doesn't mean death, though it can. It's more complicated than that."

I swallowed. The babble of the room faded away into nothing until all I heard was the sound of my own blood pumping in my ears.

"This is a card about endings, not the actual death of a person. It encourages you to allow the old to go out and let the new come in to make way for growth and transition. The card shows us that a new cycle is ahead for you, Poppy. It wants you to release your attachment to what was and welcome the transformation ahead."

"Um, okay," I murmured, still transfixed by the terrible sight of the skeleton.

"Death of dreams, perhaps," Eloise said from behind me. I turned to see her staring at the card with an odd expression on her face. I hadn't heard her join us, but I wondered if she was thinking about her career. Had she once dreamed of being a famous baker and now found herself turning out croissants in an inn kitchen while a celebrity baking show was being filmed so near to her? That could be tough. I was even more grateful now that she'd put her own concerns aside to help me.

Hamish tapped my arm. "Poppy, what was your question?"

I gulped and then couldn't help but laugh. "If I could survive bread week!"

Eloise said, "Why don't you draw another card?"

"A good idea, dear," Eve replied.

Darius excused himself and said he'd have to get back to the bar.

A little reluctantly, I took another card and turned it over. At the center of the card was a giant wheel, filled with symbols I didn't understand. Outside the wheel were an angel, eagle, bull and lion, each with wings.

"Ooh, The Wheel of Fortune," Florence said.

"That sounds better." I hoped the wheel of fortune would put a good spin on my immediate future, but Eve looked serious. She played with her long, gray braid.

"The Wheel of Fortune is reversed." I saw what she meant. I'd pulled the card and placed it so it was upside down. But did that really matter? However, looking at Eve's face, I got the feeling it did.

Florence let out her breath. "Goodness, Poppy, whatever is on your mind is a real bummer."

Eve's green eyes filled with worry, and I held her gaze, not daring to ask what it meant.

"This is one of the most highly symbolic cards in the deck. In its reverse form, The Wheel of Fortune means that luck has not been on your side and misfortunes have been following you."

"You can say that again. Poppy's always nearby when misfortune strikes around here," Hamish said. "But what if it's not as bad as it sounds? When tragedy does strike, you're the one to put things right."

I appreciated Hamish's optimism, but the sinking feeling in my belly that had slowly been spreading around my body like a poison was deepening. "What else?" I asked Eve.

"This card chimes with the death card. It's about understanding when things are beyond your control. Like the wheel, our luck and our fate are always in motion, and sometimes we are on the bottom."

Eve reached out to touch my hand, and I tried my best not to react to the energy that raced up my arm. The electric jolt was like the world's forces aligning to send me a warning. Was my destiny completely out of my control?

"Some things can't be moved by human will and action alone, dearie. The card asks you not to blame yourself. When we learn to accept, we also learn to forgive ourselves, and the wheel will turn forward again."

Florence told me not to worry and then asked Eve a final question. "What card did Darius draw, by the way?"

"The Love card," Eve replied with a grin.

CHAPTER 3

*T*hat night, skeletons, wheels, and lions danced in my dreams. I was being chased by a shapeless darkness, like an oppressive shadow trying to attach itself to mine. I woke hot and tangled in the sheets, brought back to consciousness by Gateau mewing into my ear. My eyes flicked open, and Gateau pressed her wet little nose to mine.

"Thank you, my sweet," I whispered, drawing her closer. She nuzzled into my arms, and we lay like that, both breathing deeply, until my heartbeat regulated again and she began to purr.

"That tarot reading really got under my skin," I said, shivering despite the warmth of the covers. I rolled over and checked my watch. It was only five a.m. I groaned. Gateau snuggled in closer, and I closed my eyes, willing sleep to return, minus the ghouls and terror.

I WOKE with a start when the alarm buzzed and was surprised to find Gateau still fast asleep on my chest. It was both a comforting and disquieting sight. Gateau might fall asleep with me, but she was always gone by the morning—scampering out the window to prowl the grounds and patrol the gardens. I couldn't remember a single time that she'd spent the whole night. I stroked the soft fur of her belly. "Do I need protection at the moment, sweet kitty? Is that why you've stayed?" Gateau yawned and stretched out her little paws. "Am I boring you with my worries? I guess I'll try to be more interesting from now on."

I might have affected a lighthearted tone for my familiar, but my heart was truly heavy—giant stone kind of heavy. I couldn't help but feel that the cards last night were warning me—just like the warning note I'd mysteriously received two weeks back and the ominous way both my birth dad and mom had been communicating with me only to tell me to stay away from this place. And yet I was compelled to keep returning.

Now even the tarot cards were warning me off.

If I took a step back and looked honestly at everything that had happened since I'd first set foot in Broomewode Village, then the picture was bleak. I'd come face-to-face with murder, deceit and disaster more times than anyone should in their entire lives, let alone a few weeks. Everyone and everything I encountered seemed to be telling me to leave this place, stop seeking answers, or that I was in mortal danger. Not exactly the experience I'd hoped for when I applied to be on a televised baking show when the worst disaster I could foresee was having my chocolate soufflé fall.

I dislodged Gateau from her resting place and leaned over

to the bedside table to retrieve the amethyst necklace Elspeth Peach had given me for protection. I felt the magic she'd imbued it with when I picked up the pretty crystal. If the cards were right, I was going to be needing this more than ever. I held the necklace in my hand and closed my eyes, trying to tap into the power of my sisters living here, where there was said to be an energy vortex.

I was feeling my power, Gateau's fur soft under my hand, when a voice said, "Did you call me?"

I opened my eyes. "Gerry. What are you doing here?"

The moment was shattered as Gateau reared up and scampered away towards the window. My familiar and ghostly Gerry never seemed to get along. He looked puzzled. "I dunno. I was down at the tent thinking about knocking Hamish's yeast to the ground and moving Florence's ingredients around. She gets really flustered when everything's not exactly in the proper order. But then I felt like you were holding on to the back of my shirt and pulling me. Next thing I knew, I was here."

Honestly, I was as shocked as Gerry. He kept trying to move on but wasn't having any luck. Was it me holding him here? Even though I didn't need him or even particularly want him with me?

It was another mystery.

I started to tell him about the tarot card reading when he stopped me. "I know. Heard all about it. Florence and that waiter bloke were talking about it."

"Florence and Darius were talking about my death card?"

"Yep. Said you were doomed. That's why I wanted to mess up her cooking station a bit."

"I appreciate the support, but why chuck Hamish's yeast to the floor? Has he done something to annoy you?"

"As a matter of fact, he has. He gets to hang about with you and Florence with his 'wee dram o' Scottish charm.'" The last bit was said in a broad imitation of a Scottish accent that had me laughing. But I stopped when he continued. "And I'm stuck watching it all and never able to join in. It's like I'm invisible."

Since I had no answer for that, I told him I had to get ready.

He nodded. Usually he had some new trick to show me or he'd talk to me while hanging from the ceiling, or push just his head through my wall and have a conversation, but not today. He looked serious. "Pops, I'm worried about you. I'll stay with you in the tent and keep my eyes open for danger, but you know I can't stop a bullet, even if I want to."

I was genuinely touched and also unnerved that Gerry believed I was in danger. "The cards aren't meant to be taken literally," I assured him and tried to reassure myself. "Don't listen to Florence. You know what a drama queen she is."

"Don't be too trusting, Poppy."

Not having time to hear his theories, I told him I had to get ready and he needed to leave. He melted through the door with a quiet dignity that I found disturbing. Where were his crazy antics today?

I hopped in the shower and tried to scrub away the feeling of doom. Yet another Saturday morning had rolled around without me feeling rested or ready for the challenges ahead. All I could do was hope that Eloise's expertise had sunk into my sludgy brain or that my hands would reflexively remember how to knead dough. I was relying on my last-minute cramming session just like a teenager staying up all night before an exam. *Great work, Pops.*

I stood under the shower an extra-long time, then dragged my weary body out, toweled off, and wrapped my wet hair in a turban.

Gina had tried to lend me a gorgeous green maxi dress with wide straps and a simple white T-shirt to go underneath, but I couldn't handle it. For my ordeal by bread, I'd chosen a favorite sky-blue T-shirt over comfortable white slacks. Florence always looked glamorous, and I couldn't compete. I hoped, when viewers watched me, they'd appreciate my down-to-earth style. Was down-to-earth even an actual style?

I went to the wardrobe and almost dropped my towel when I found Gerry standing stock-still, his crazy shirt patterned with cars and trucks at the same level as my shirts.

"You scared me," I said, as he burst out laughing. "That was NOT funny. I nearly had a heart attack."

He was obviously feeling better and had rid himself of the gloomy mood. Thank goodness.

I'd been feeling seriously guilty about not helping Gerry pass over to the other side, and in between bread-making, I'd decided to consult Susan and Eve to formulate some kind of plan to get him moving. However, I wondered when I'd find time. Maybe after the bread-baking weekend.

I took my clothes from the wardrobe and then barricaded myself in the bathroom to change, warning Gerry that now was not the time to float through any walls. He so did not want to get on my bad side today.

Through the door, I told Gerry that I was worried that bread week might be the death of me. "Maybe that's what the death card meant."

"Really?" Gerry replied. "But bread is easy. If I hadn't been murdered the first week, I'd have aced bread week." He was overlooking the tiny detail that he'd been sent home after the first episode, so he wouldn't have aced bread week live or dead.

"Bread's not easy for me," I told him.

"But seriously, Poppy, you've got to pull yourself together. You can't be voted off the show. What will I do for companionship? Talk to the walls?"

In spite of his self-centered reasoning, I felt for him. "Believe me, I'm trying my best." I emerged from the bathroom, dressed and towel-drying my hair.

"Ooh, you look nice," Gerry said. "Comfortable."

As I plugged in my hair dryer, he said, "Are you planning to woo Jonathon Pine with your wily feminine charms and hope that he doesn't notice your bread is as solid as a rock?"

"Eww, don't talk about Jonathon that way. He could be my dad."

I paused for a moment. Oh my goodness. Could Jonathon Pine actually be my dad? Was that where I'd inherited my love of baking? Was I being crazy? Yes. I was being crazy.

Gerry said, "Since I'm brilliant at making bread, I've decided to accompany you to the tent and walk you through everything you need to do. But I can only help so much. Bread-making is about instinct and touch, feeling your way through the process. Since I can't actually feel anything, think of me as your spiritual bread guru."

Oh man, I did not need to add to my stress levels today.

"Oh, Gerry, that's kind, but please stay here today. You've no idea how hard it is to pretend not to see you when the cameras are rolling. It'll only distract me more."

"Fine," he said. "I'll have to be your cheerleader from afar."

I told Gerry I appreciated it, and after he wished me luck, I raced downstairs for breakfast.

Gaurav and Maggie were at the buffet, and I joined them, helping myself to scrambled eggs and a side of crispy bacon. There was whole-grain toast, Danish and croissants I knew Eloise had crafted in the kitchen early this morning. I looked at the breads and saw doom. No bread for me this morning.

Hamish gave me an awkward pat on the shoulder as I sat down. "Ready for another good show?" he asked.

"No. Maybe we should be like actors and say 'break a leg.'"

He shook his head. "With your luck, you'll fall down and snap your femur. I'll stick with 'have a good show.'"

Oh, great. Now I had something else to worry about.

Everyone else seemed well rested and happy to chat jovially as if bread week were no big deal. I kept my head down and shoveled eggs into my mouth. Before long, Florence swept into the room.

"You look resplendent, darling," Maggie cooed.

Maggie was right, although we'd all come to expect nothing less from Florence's on-screen appearances. Today she was wearing a vintage-looking silk skirt and matching shirt in dramatic black. The shirt had sweet little cap sleeves, and she'd swept her hair up into a tumbling updo. Large drop pearl earrings swung from her lobes. It was more femme fatale than baking babe, but that was Florence. Hamish and Gaurav were both in T-shirts and jeans, and Maggie was wearing a peach floral shirt and cream linen trousers. The weather was predicted to be hot. And I knew I'd be hot and bothered in more ways than just the soaring temperature.

We finished our breakfast and were about to leave for the tent when Eve caught my eye and asked to have a quiet word. Oh great, was I about to get more words of warning from my coven sister?

"Good luck today, Poppy," she said, touching my arm so I could feel her energy adding to mine. "I've been feeling guilty about the tarot reading last night. Please don't worry about that death card. You know it's only a bit of fun, and the death card usually only means that change is coming."

"I know, but I'd rather have had one of those that tell you a large sum of money is coming your way, along with a tall, dark and handsome stranger."

"Go on with you," she said, laughing. "You do your best and you'll be fine."

I tried to assure her that I was fine even though I so was not. "The death card might mean change is coming, but sometimes it does actually mean death is around the corner, right? Whatever way you look at it, it doesn't bode well for the competition this weekend. I can't get it out of my mind."

Eve frowned. "I was worried the cards might spook you, but I don't think it means you're in any danger." She paused and looked down at her wrist. "Here," she said, unclasping a bracelet. "This is my protection amulet." She pressed a sleek silver bracelet into my hand. It was shiny and smooth, with an oval purple stone set into its center. "It's amethyst," she said, "like your necklace from Elspeth. Wear the two charms together and you'll be doubly safe."

She fastened the clasp and smiled broadly. "Perfect fit."

She glanced around to make sure we couldn't be overheard, then, clasping my hands in hers, recited,

> *Goddesses of Sun, Earth, Stars and Moon,*
> *Protect this woman from night to noon*
> *Evil keep away, I hereby command.*
> *In safety and comfort, Goddesses, hold her in your hand.*
> *So I will, so mote it be.*

I did feel better knowing my sisters were looking out for me. The bracelet felt good on my wrist. "This makes me feel better. I promise to look after it."

I ran to catch up with the others. I had the amethyst necklace from Elspeth, a protection amulet from Eve; all I needed now was a pair of earrings and I'd have a full set.

CHAPTER 4

he moment I stepped inside *The Great British Baking Contest's* famous white tent, my nerves flooded right back. I went straight to Gina's chair, more in need of her own brand of magic than I'd ever been before.

"The casual look suits you," Gina said, surprising me. She took a step back and cast an appraising eye over me. I'd pulled my hair back in a simple ponytail to keep it out of my way and off my neck. I thought she'd criticize or try to change it, but instead she said, "You look awfully pale, Pops." She peered at me. "Those dark circles. Yikes." She shook her head. "What have I told you about getting a good night's rest before filming? There's only so much concealer can do."

I hung my head and told her that I'd been worrying so much about this weekend, I couldn't relax.

"Oh, Pops, you need to settle down. You're a nervous wreck."

I wanted to tell Gina that I was certain this week was going to be the end of me, maybe in more ways than one, but I didn't want to pass on my negative energy. Instead, I mustered up a smile and said that if I survived today, I'd rest tonight.

She raised a brow. "Survive? Don't be so dramatic."

I cracked and told her about Eve's tarot reading and how I'd been dealt the death card. But Gina just laughed it off. "Come on, Pops. Everyone knows tarot is baloney."

I was surprised at how easily Gina dismissed the reading. Not for the first time, I wished that I could share with her the part of my life as a water witch, explain how Eve was intuitive about this world and the next. But of course, I had to keep my mouth shut.

Gina whipped out her makeup tool kit and got to work on my face. It took everything I had not to fall asleep in the chair, but after fifteen minutes, she declared me done. I stared into her handheld mirror and grinned. "You really are the best," I said, admiring my carefully lined eyes and new pink pout.

"And don't you forget it. Now go get 'em. I've every faith you're going to be brilliant."

I hugged Gina close, wishing I could draw in some of her confidence.

I walked to my workstation like I was walking the plank. I lined up my ingredients and stared at them solemnly. Robbie, the sound guy, came over to test my mike. "You feeling all right?"

"Nervous. Very."

Robbie assured me that I'd be fine. "Not that my opinion counts for much around here, but I think you're in with a chance of winning this thing."

"That's sweet, but you haven't seen my soda bread yet."

Robbie laughed and told me I'd be fine. Didn't they

realize that someone was voted off the show each week? That someone *had* to go?

Fiona, the director, stood at the front of the tent and called for everyone's attention. She warned us that it was due to be scorching hot today and so she'd ordered desk fans for everyone's workstation to try to keep us cool—and help us keep our cool.

"How thoughtful," Florence whispered to me. "I couldn't bear it if my makeup began to run."

Normally I'd laugh at Florence's concerns, but today I knew that I needed my makeup to stay put too. No one wanted to watch a pale ghost baking. Speaking of pale ghosts, I glanced around, but Gerry had listened to me. I saw his form on the outside of the tent. He was peering in, looking around as though he were on security detail. I turned away before he spotted me and thought I wanted him to come closer.

One of the show's runners, a young girl named Tina who I'd only seen once or twice before, delivered the fans. She turned mine on for me and blushed when I thanked her. She looked as overwhelmed as I was to be on set. I put on my clean apron and tried to look confident, happy, in control.

Once everyone was settled again, Fiona called for quiet. There was this moment right before she called for action when the world seemed unnaturally still and silent. *You've got this,* I told myself, searching for calm. I could see Jonathon and Elspeth ready and the two comedians already looking as though they were about to crack a joke.

The cameras were set up, the scent of freshly baked Victoria sponge faintly discernible. And then several things seemed to happen at once. Fiona yelled "Action." Elspeth and

Jonathon began to walk forward. An urge to run came to me from nowhere, but before my feet could move, a powerful force shoved me so hard, I was propelled backward until I hit Florence's workstation.

I saw the big lights above my station fall before the tent shook with the ear-splitting sound of them crashing exactly where I'd been standing.

"What the—?" I murmured, stunned, but my words were drowned out by Florence's scream.

Where I'd been standing seconds before, the big overhead light had come loose from the rigging and tumbled down, shattering on the tent's pine floor.

Florence rushed to my side as the cameras filmed us. "My dearest friend," she cried, holding me to her bosom. "You were nearly killed."

I couldn't respond. My heart was beating wildly, and all I could focus on was getting back my breath. Suddenly everyone was gathered around me. Hamish's voice asked if I was okay. The crowd was suffocating. What had happened? One minute I was standing still, and the next, it was like my legs didn't belong to me. How had I moved so quickly? I certainly hadn't seen that great light coming towards me. For a terrible moment, I thought I might faint. How embarrassing to black out in the competition tent, but then my words started to return to me, and I let them tumble out. "I'm okay... not hurt...narrow miss..."

I felt as if I'd been pushed, but no one had been close enough. Then I saw Gerry, floating above the crowd, looking as worried as a ghost can. In the babble of voices talking to me, I replied, the words intended for my guardian ghost. "I'm fine. Thank you."

It was Gina's worried face that really brought me back to life. She looked at me searchingly. "Poppy, I should have taken your fears more seriously." She looked as shaken as I felt. She pulled me close and whispered into my ear. "I shouldn't have laughed when you said you were worried. You've always had a sixth sense for danger. You were right. I'm so sorry."

But I shook my head and murmured she had nothing to apologize for. Not in a million years did I think that the danger was going to be a wayward set light. Despite the heat, I suddenly went cold. It was exactly like the time I'd been picking gooseberries on Susan Bentley's farm. One minute, everything was fine. The next, a massive tumbling rock headed straight in my direction. If Sly, Susan's gorgeous border collie, hadn't been with me, that thing would have flattened me for sure. It was only his barking that alerted me and his careful herding (with the help of my sweet Gateau) that got me out of harm's way.

I didn't know how Gerry had done it or if he'd had help from Elspeth and Eve with their protection spells, but I was safe.

"I don't understand," Fiona was saying. "We run a tight ship here. That light should never have been able to come loose like that. Everything is checked and double-checked. Triple-checked even! Especially after that awful fiasco with the ovens."

"Clearly not checked properly," Florence cried out, a hand to her heart. "She could have been killed."

She definitely had a great career ahead of her as an actress. "It was an accident," I murmured. "No one's fault."

But it didn't feel like an accident. It felt like Death was

37

coming straight for me. Just like the cards had foretold. I shivered. Was I overreacting? Or had the fates aligned to warn me of my impending death?

I realized everyone was still crowded around, talking a mile a minute.

"She's had a shock," Maggie said, putting her capable hand on my forehead as though I were a grandchild running a fever. "Can someone get her a cup of sweet tea?"

"Good idea," Fiona said, looking determined. "Everyone, take a break while we get this mess cleaned up. Where's the electrician?" she barked. I didn't envy whoever had signed off on those lights.

Robbie appeared with a stool, and I took a seat. Tina, the runner, handed me a cup of hot tea. I gingerly blew across the surface and then took a sip. It was sweet and reviving. I thanked everyone and said I was feeling much better. I took a few more sips of tea and then stood up. I felt wobbly at first—whatever had moved my legs so fast had exhausted them—but I stayed standing. "The show must go on, right?" I said to Florence, trying my best to smile wholeheartedly.

"That's what we say in show business," she replied. I looked around for Gerry, but he'd disappeared. However, Hamish and Gaurav both stood near as though they might be needed. Maggie asked if I wanted a nurse, and once again, I insisted I was all right.

After the mess had been swept away and a new lighting arrangement made, Fiona said that we were ready to shoot.

Elspeth remained in the corner of the tent with Jonathon, Arty and Jilly. She cast me worried glances but didn't come near. I wanted desperately to ask her if the force I felt pushing me out of harm's way was magical. Had Elspeth intervened from afar?

I caught her eye, and she mouthed, "Are you okay?" across the tent. I nodded. But all I wanted was to curl up and go back to bed. I couldn't shake the feeling that something was terribly wrong, that the light falling was no accident. If only I could sleep the day away and wake tomorrow afternoon with the weekend's bread challenges behind me. *Yeah, right, as if anything on this show is ever that easy.*

Elspeth gave me a warm smile and a knowing look as if to say that all was well; don't let this distract you. She came to the front of the tent, readying herself. She wore a cream linen suit and gold earrings and looked calm and beautiful. And now that she stood closer to my station, the calmer I began to feel, too.

After I'd finished my tea, Gina redid my lips and applied a little blusher to my cheeks.

We resumed our places, and I tried to ignore the recently patched floor at my feet.

Fiona yelled, "Action!" and I tried not to wince.

I trained my focus on Jilly as she introduced bread week, but her words floated over me. Nothing sank in. It was like I was underwater, descending down to the ocean's bed. I wouldn't have even noticed it was time to start baking if Arty's dreadful pun hadn't penetrated my fog.

"Now guys, remember, when the doughing gets tough, the tough get doughing. On your marks, get set, bake!"

And so the first baking round began. We had ninety minutes to create and bake a soda bread, and I had to work fast.

My first step was to caramelize the onions. Great. A

vegetable that could make you cry—so not what I needed right now. I started by slicing the onion and sweating it in extra virgin olive oil for a rich, intense flavor. Once it was soft, I added balsamic vinegar and a smattering of soft, light brown sugar. While it was simmering, I began to weigh out my dry ingredients. So far so good.

Above me, a familiar figure floated. I knew Gerry was watching out for me, but I had to concentrate extra hard not to glance his way and talk to him.

I kept my head down and took out my frustration on the cheese grater. Of course, this was the exact moment Arty and Jonathon decided to approach.

"So Poppy," Jonathon said, clearing his throat, "I can see you're playing it safe here with a classic combination of caramelized onions and cheddar."

I swallowed. Was this a criticism or simply an observation?

"That's right," I replied. "Bread-making doesn't come so naturally to me, so I'm putting my faith in quality ingredients and a good flavor combo to guide me through."

"Admitting your weaknesses to the great Jonathon Pine?" Arty said. "Bold move."

Except that I wasn't feeling bold at all. I was still spooked from the falling light, and the image of the death card invaded my mind's eye. Besides, I couldn't tell Arty (and the millions of viewers at home) that I didn't mind admitting my weaknesses to Jonathon because I'd stumbled upon him memorizing his lines.

The nerves (real terror) must have shown in my face, because something in Jonathon softened. "Nothing wrong with making a classic well," he said. "Execute this perfectly, and it could be a stunner."

Clearly Jonathon had never tasted my bread. But I thanked him, and they left to torture another contestant.

"Come on, Pops," Gerry said in a cheerleading tone, "almost time to knead that dough. Let me see your knuckles in action."

Argh, why couldn't Gerry just float off. I realized I was frowning and tried to arrange my feature into a neutral expression and, with my onions now cool, added them along with the cheese into the flour mix.

"Not sure you caramelized those onions for long enough, Pops," Gerry said.

That comment was so not helpful now that they were in my bowl and covered in flour. I carefully poured out my buttermilk, and a dough began to form.

"Handle it gently," Gerry whispered.

As if I was going to bash it and throw it across the room.

"Jeez. It's not your worst enemy," he continued.

No, but I know who might be ...

I carefully shaped it into a ball, recalling Eloise's guiding hands and gentle instructions yesterday.

But Gerry wouldn't stop interfering. "*Gently* does it," he repeated. I felt my hands tense, irritation flowing through me.

"Don't bloody squeeze it, Pops!" he exclaimed.

Argh. Gerry had to go, and since I couldn't shout at him with millions of viewers watching, then I was going to have to find another way. I rounded the dough into a ball and cut a cross into the middle ... and then I walked right through Gerry.

"OOOhhh no, that did not feel good," he said.

I couldn't resist a little smirk.

"Okay, I get it," Gerry said, pouting. "I'll watch from afar."

Smug, I added a sprinkle of cheese on the top for a chewy crust, and then it was time to take it to the oven.

I wished my soda bread well and closed the door with a sigh. Hopefully, in thirty-five minutes, I'd have a golden soda bread to be proud of. At least I'd managed to keep the timing under control. As had everyone else. I looked around, and the other bakers were either walking to or from the oven with their breads. So far, no disasters to be seen, no cries of anguish to be heard. With only five competitors left, the stakes were high. We were all used to the tent, to the cameras and the equipment, to the commentary of the judges and the jibes of the comedians. It was going to take more than Arty's childish sense of humor to throw us off our game. But instead of finding this reassuring, I realized that I had no excuses. Everyone left in the competition was strong and assured. Everyone, that is, except me. I so did not want to be toast this week.

I returned to my workstation with my heart in my throat and tackled the floury mess I'd made across the white surfaces. But I couldn't shake the feeling that something bad was about to happen. Now that the bread was made, I kept finding myself looking skyward, as if another light were about to take me out. But it was more than just the dodgy light. I was beset with the feeling that something, or some-one, was coming for me. I just didn't know what or where. It put me on edge.

I was so busy with thoughts of doom that I'd forgotten to check on my bread. I let out a yelp of distress, which in turn alerted the cameras to potential drama. They followed me as I dashed to the oven. I wrenched open the door.

"Phew," I whispered. The bread was fine. It had risen and puffed out. The cheese was perhaps a little crispy, but it wasn't burnt to cinders—and for that I was grateful. Like drop down to my knees and thank the baking gods kind of grateful.

I removed my cheesy soda bread from the oven as Jilly called out that we had five minutes remaining.

I'd brought a beautiful wooden board from home to present my bread. It had been a Christmas present from my parents and was made by a craftsman from their village in Provence. I loved its sweeping grain and the small, darker knots of wood that spoke of the material's past life as an old, grand tree. I arranged my bread on its surface carefully, frowning a little where the curls of cheese had crisped. Oh well. It certainly wasn't the worst loaf I'd ever baked.

When Jilly asked us to bring our loaves to the judging table, I felt numb. Yes, I was relieved that the morning's task was over, but did I think my loaf was going to stand out when set against Maggie's delightful pecan and chocolate bread? Nope. Or Gaurav's beautiful pink beetroot and caraway concoction? No sirree. Not a chance.

I couldn't even bring myself to focus on the judging. It took all my control to just keep myself from grimacing on camera.

When Jonathon sliced my loaf, he looked to Elspeth, as he so often did during judging.

"Well, from the looks of it, Poppy, you didn't quite caramelize the onions enough," she said.

Oh man, Gerry was right—how galling.

"And you might have skimped a little on the cheese, too," Jonathon added.

"Let's see, shall we?" Elspeth interrupted and took a delicate bite. I watched and waited. The seconds ticked by, each one feeling longer than the last.

Elspeth swallowed. "It's a little underwhelming, I'm afraid."

Jonathon nodded. "Not enough sweetness from the onions, not enough cheese. The dough feels like it's been overworked, too."

"I'm afraid I have to agree." Elspeth looked at me sadly. "Not your best effort, Poppy."

My heart sank into my sneakers.

When judging ended, all my worst fears came true. I was bottom of the pile.

CHAPTER 5

*A*s I waited in line for lunch, Elspeth's words echoed in my head. *Not your best effort, Poppy. Not your best effort.* The words stung, not because they were untrue—my bread was pretty sad—but it was the idea that I hadn't put in enough *effort* that hurt. I had tried—oh, how I'd tried—to master bread. Hours and hours of practice. Boring Mildred, my kitchen ghost, Gina, and even going so far as to enlist the help of a professional at the inn. But it hadn't worked. All attempts to master this elusive bake had been thwarted. It was only the first of three, I reminded myself. I could bounce back from this.

I wished hard that I could blame my poor turnout this morning on the lighting rig's attempt on my life, but deep down I knew that this week I'd reached the limitations of my baking skills. It was going to take a miracle for me to get through this weekend—not to mention get through to the next round of the competition.

I was so bogged down in my own doom and gloom that I'd barely registered that Maggie had come first in the signa-

45

ture bake section. Perhaps I wouldn't have noticed at all if it wasn't for how Florence was sulking next to me. Although she spoke only words of praise for Maggie, her puffy bottom lip jutted out and betrayed her real feelings. I could tell that she'd thought her bread was going to take first place.

I couldn't have been paying Florence enough attention because she abruptly broke off her monologue and gawped at me. "Poppy? Are you in there?"

"I hope so," I half joked. "I'm not on top of my game today."

Florence looked as if she were about to protest and then said, "You had a dreadful shock this morning. This afternoon you'll do better."

Oh, great, not even Florence could act her way through pretending I was any good this morning.

I had pasta salad—I so could not stomach a sandwich right now, not with its fluffy baked white loaf taunting me with its perfect texture. I was glad there were no hot options today. Even though it was only midday, the sun was burning its way through the clear blue sky. I was worried about the technical challenge to come; I was already hot under the collar without the weather adding to my woes. It was going to be impossible to keep cool. At least lunch would provide the fuel I needed to get through the rest of the day.

"I'm not sure you could fit much more on that plate," a low voice said teasingly.

I spun round, ready to snap the head off anyone who dared to comment on my food consumption. To my surprise, it was Benedict. And he had such a warm look on his face that any budding vitriol about to pour forth dissipated immediately and I laughed instead.

"I'm glad to see you laughing," Benedict said, looking worried. "I heard about the accident on set this morning. I came up here to make sure you were okay."

Now I really was stumped for words. Benedict and I had certainly got off on the wrong foot when we first met—I mean, talking to someone as if he were a restless spirit, devising ways to sneak around his home, and then accusing his father of murder was not going to endear me to anyone. But since he saved my life last week, knocking down the terrible old gamekeeper before he let rip with his rifle, I wondered if perhaps he didn't find me as annoying as he did before. And for my part, perhaps I'd jumped to unfair conclusions about Benedict. He'd been pretty normal the last couple of weeks. Or was I simply getting used to him? Maybe he wasn't the stuck-up heir of Broomewode Hall I'd assumed he was.

But before I could answer, Florence jumped in, all but pushing me aside as she rushed to tell the story. "Poppy got the death card in a tarot reading last night. Maybe you should stay close and keep an eye on all of us."

Florence flicked her hair over her shoulders, a trick I'd seen her use on pretty much every guy we encountered. Was she actually flirting with Benedict? He was a good catch, after all. He had a title, a mansion, and he wasn't exactly ugly, if you went for the tall, dark and handsome type.

Benedict looked at me expectantly, and I realized I'd yet to say a word about the accident. I decided to claim I'd had plenty of time to jump out of the way, not that some mysterious force had propelled me away from disaster.

"Since the accident happened on Broomewode grounds, I will certainly look into it," Benedict said.

Oh. So that was it. Benedict was afraid of damaging the family reputation. Go figure.

I thanked him and said I'd have to eat before the technical challenge kicked off.

"Poppy can really put food away," Florence commented. "Not that you'd know from the size of her."

Benedict looked at me and then back at Florence. "A healthy appetite is an admirable quality," he said, and then bade us both goodbye.

I smiled a little sheepishly, pleased that Benedict had stood up for me in his own weird way.

Back in the tent, the heat was rising. I could see that everyone was worried about baking in these temperatures. I was so glad I'd dressed for comfort. Florence was anxious about her makeup slipping, Hamish that his dripping forehead would accidentally oversalt his bread. But I knew that it was me that was in real danger. Again, I thought back to Eve drawing that death card from the pack. What did it mean? Had the card been warning me about the accident this morning? I hoped so, because then the card would have done its job and I could let it go.

There had also been the upside down wheel of fortune, and that had definitely come true as well. I was absolutely at the bottom of the wheel and had to work hard to get myself up again. I didn't need to win this competition. I only had to bake better than one other person. To do that, I was going to have to pull myself together. Starting now.

The judges and comedians entered the tent, and Fiona called, "Action." The technical bake had arrived.

Here we go again. I glanced up nervously. No swinging light. *Don't be paranoid, Pops.*

Jonathon Pine was known for his bread. Whether it was bagels, rye, or farmhouse loaf, bread was his thing. I'd already disappointed both judges in the signature round, and now I needed to shine. On my workstation, a group of ingredients and kit were covered with a dishcloth. I trembled just looking at it.

"Good afternoon, bakers," Jonathon said, taking a step forward. It was already really sticky in the tent, and I felt the sweat gathering on my lower back. I was so glad I had a second, identical shirt for tomorrow. "Today's technical challenge is a chocolate and hazelnut babka."

A what? I looked around—did anyone else know what a babka was? Florence and Maggie were smiling and nodding, but Hamish and Gaurav appeared to be as perplexed as I was. At least I wasn't completely alone in my babka ignorance. How was I going to make a bread I'd never heard of? What should it look like? How should it taste?

"For those of you who need a little history lesson, I'm going to be kind," Jonathon said.

Jonathon Pine being kind? Now that was a turnup for the books.

"A babka is a sweet braided bread which originated in the Jewish communities of Poland and Ukraine," he continued.

Okay, but what does it look like? Thick or thin braids? A loaf shape or circular? I could *feel* the hush fall over the tent as we waited impatiently for more details.

"That's all the info you'll be getting from me. Now it's up to you to follow the instructions and get those babkas baked."

Oh. Great. It's a braided sweet bread. I needed way more than that to get going!

"Seize the dough, bakers," Arty said. "You have an hour and a half, and your time starts now."

I lifted the dishcloth and stared at the ingredients as if they might come to life and tell me what to do. I'd never heard of a babka, so I was going to have to follow Jonathon's instructions very carefully. To my horror, the sheet had seventeen steps.

"Don't let the long list put you off." It was Gerry. "Just get cracking."

Okay, for once Gerry was right—even if he was explicitly going against my instructions to buzz off. "Do you know what a babka is?" I asked him, hoping it looked like I was reading the instructions to myself.

"Sure," he said, sounding confident. "It should look like a rectangle with rounded ends."

I tipped the hazelnuts into a baking tray and put them into the oven to roast. So far, so good. A few minutes later, they were the light golden color Jonathon had instructed, so I let them cool and then split them into two piles—one to be roughly chopped and the other finely chopped.

"Good work, Pops," Gerry said.

Now for the chocolate part. I placed the butter, sugar and chocolate in a pan and let it melt very slowly over a low heat. As I stirred the mixture, I noticed my hand was shaking. *Get it together, Pops.* "You're doing fine," Gerry said. For once actually helping.

Jonathon and Elspeth arrived at Florence's workstation, and in her bright, confident voice, I heard her explaining more about babkas.

"My Nona used to make a babka every time we visited her in Italy at Eastertime. She made hers with cinnamon and sugar, rather than chocolate, but the concept is the same. To me, babkas are a taste of home."

Oh, great, so Florence was a babka expert. What chance did that leave a novice like me?

"That's a heartwarming story," Elspeth said, smiling. "Did you help her in the kitchen?"

Florence nodded, her eyes bright and sparkling. She was in her element, the cameras zooming in, following her every move. "She taught me how to twist the yeasty dough around itself so that it curled a bit like a shy snake."

Elspeth laughed. "I like that, a shy snake indeed."

Jonathon wished Florence luck, though clearly Lady Luck was already on her side, having a party for one.

The two judges approached me.

I swallowed and took my melted chocolate off the heat.

"How are you getting on?" Elspeth asked, a kindness in her voice that almost brought a tear to my eye.

"Okay, I think," I confessed, "but that's because I haven't got to the dough part yet."

"Have you ever made a babka before?" Jonathon asked.

I shook my head. "I'm not the expert like my neighbor." I gestured to Florence, who grinned. "But I'm hoping for a little beginner's luck."

The judges smiled and left to speak to Hamish. Phew. That was short and sweet.

Now for the dough. From the instructions, I could see that it was yeast-heavy, which Eloise explained to me yesterday would make bread sticky to work with. And this is where Jonathon's instructions became more complicated. I had to add the yeast to one side of the bowl and sugar and salt to the other. I switched on the mixer, made a well in the center and poured in the eggs and milk. I stopped. The dough was supposed to be firm. Wasn't it? I lifted the bowl to eye level. Was that firm enough? I couldn't tell. I didn't trust my instincts.

Gerry couldn't touch it, so he didn't know either. "Looks all right," he said.

I increased the speed and went to add the butter already measured out in a bowl. But the heat made my fingers sweaty and I was nervous to boot.

The bowl slipped out of my hands. *Stop.* I pointed my finger at the bowl as though it was a human wand, and the bowl hovered in space, but then two things hit me at once. I wasn't allowed to use magic for improper purposes, and a camera was catching the whole disaster. Letting that bowl of butter fall when I could have saved it was one of the hardest things I'd ever done. It fell to the floor with a splintering crash. My second of the day.

"Whoa, there, butterfingers," Arty called out into the deafening silence.

I glanced down at the pieces of the broken bowl. My butter had splattered everywhere.

"Plenty more where that came from," Elspeth said. She was suddenly by my side, cradling a bowl of butter in her arms like a newborn. "Just take it slowly," she advised. "You've got time. Don't rush this."

I nodded.

"And well done on not using your magic," she whispered. "That was well done."

I took the butter gratefully, and stood aside as an assistant cleaned up the mess I'd made. Then I continued with the babka. The dough was sticky, but I let the mixer do its thing until it became a ball of smooth, silky, shiny dough.

I spread the cooled chocolate mixture over the dough, sprinkled the hazelnuts, and then it was time to roll the dough into a tight spiral. This was the part I'd been dreading. I needed to be dexterous and neat. But my fingers felt like carrot stumps, and I couldn't get the dough to obey. I pulled it this way and that as I tried to get the seam underneath.

"That should have been in the oven already," Gerry whispered.

I didn't know why he was whispering when I was the only one who could hear him. But I blocked out the noise and kept my head down. *Just get through this, Pops.*

I cut and twisted, making a two-strand plait, pressed, and repeated, and then sealed the lot. I stood back. It was a mess, but there was nothing for it but to slide my babka into a proving drawer. Once it had risen, I could wish it well and send it to the oven.

The remaining time passed in a blur. I made the syrup, managed not to burn the sugar, and got my babka baked.

Jilly called out five minutes, and I rushed to the oven. Everyone else had already removed their babkas from the oven and were drizzling their syrup over the top. I'd spent too long twisting the dough, and now I was behind. I could see that the babka clearly needed another few minutes, but that was time I didn't have. I opened the oven door and immediately noticed my bake wasn't as chocolatey brown as the others. What had happened?

I took it back to my workstation, and that's when I saw the pot of unused cocoa powder sitting oh so innocently on the side. I'd forgotten to put it into my mix. A silly, avoidable mistake. So now I had an underbaked, underflavored babka to present to the judges. Great.

I sprinkled cocoa over the top of the bread, which gave it a better color, and drizzled it with syrup.

"Bready or not, your time is up, bakers," Jilly called. Her huge hoop earrings swung from side to side as she gently laughed at her own pun.

It was time to take my babka to the table. Where had the ninety minutes gone? As with the morning, I couldn't bring myself to listen to the judging. It was torture, waiting to be told how poor my babka was. So naturally, my ears pricked up at the words "stodgy" and "messy," but to my amazement, they were talking about Hamish's bake.

Hamish looked mortified, and my heart went out to him. I knew exactly what it was like to hear negative feedback from the judges. It felt so personal, like they were criticizing your family. Surely once they finished praising Florence's babka, they'd come to mine and then Hamish could feel better about himself.

I waited as Elspeth sliced through my bake. "The color on this is a little..." She stopped and seemed to be searching for the right adjective. "Bland," she finally settled on.

Ouch.

"And by the looks of it, it's not had long enough in the oven," Jonathon added.

I could only nod in agreement.

Jonathon bit into the dough. "But it's not bad, exactly. Just a little underwhelming."

Whoa. Okay. Underwhelming was not an ideal adjective, but at least he hadn't written it off entirely. I'd take that.

Gaurav, who'd obviously never heard of babka either and

didn't have a ghost giving him tips, had made something long and thin that looked burned.

Jonathon complained about the shape, and Elspeth agreed. "And it tastes overbaked, rather dry," was the final verdict.

Maggie's was gorgeous, and both judges complimented her on an excellent bake.

Elspeth and Jonathon left the judging table to confer. This was the worst bit. The waiting felt endless, although in reality, I knew it only lasted a couple of minutes. I looked at my fellow bakers. Only Hamish appeared worried. He was sweating profusely, his forehead crinkled with self-doubt.

Elspeth and Jonathon returned, and it was time for the order of the babkas to be announced.

They began, as usual, with last place. I held my breath, steeling myself for the sting of my name being called. But to my surprise, Hamish was at the bottom.

He looked crumpled.

Next was Gaurav, then me, Maggie, and finally Florence was crowned the winner of the technical challenge.

I let out a huge sigh of relief. Somehow, I wasn't at the very bottom of the pack. In fact, I was smack in the middle. There was hope. But it was still going to be a long climb back up to the top. I was going to need every ounce of energy left in my body to put into my showstopper tomorrow. It would have to be spectacular—otherwise this could be my last weekend in the tent.

I left the tent and walked back with the others to the inn. The afternoon was sweltering, and all I could think about was running a cool bath and soaking the day away. Florence was giddy with her win, and Maggie was quietly confident.

Gaurav didn't seem too bothered about his babka. Only Hamish and I seemed downcast. "You always know your luck will run out," he said. "But you're never ready for it to actually happen."

"Exactly."

In the car park, I saw Eloise loading something into her car.

She waved at me and came over. I let the others go ahead and waited. "And?" she asked expectantly, when she was a couple of feet away. "How did it go? Did you nail it?"

I told her the truth, that I'd made some silly mistakes and was pretty much bottom of the pack. "I'm going to have to do something miraculous tomorrow for the showstopper to save myself."

"What are you making?"

"We have to make an edible bread sculpture. I want to do a basket of flowers as I'm a graphic designer and I've done a lot of work around gardens and flowers. It's just so hot in the tent, the bread dough got sticky and hard to deal with."

Eloise looked concerned. "Yeast loves heat. It might rise too quickly, and the flour can act like a sponge when it's humid. I've got some deliveries to make now, but why don't you pop back into the kitchen later? I've got some fresh yeast in today. We can look in the pantry for some goodies to help your bread garden."

"Thank you."

Florence suddenly appeared. She introduced herself and asked Eloise if she had any cardamom pods to spare. "I'm worried mine might be a bit stale. The Italian grocer in Broomewode promised me he had some, but they didn't come in. He's really let me down."

Eloise shook her head. "I'm afraid not," she said curtly and then excused herself.

Florence raised an eyebrow, but I only shrugged. "Cardamom pods must be in short supply."

She stared at Eloise's back as the woman strode towards the kitchen door. "Perhaps."

CHAPTER 6

I ate dinner in silence, barely participating in the evening's revelry. The relief I was used to feeling after a long Saturday baking eluded me. Florence and Gaurav were in stitches as Hamish did his impression of Jonathon Pine screwing up his nose at Hamish's babka. I was in awe of how well Hamish was handling criticism. I'd felt like I'd fallen down a deep well today and had no way of scaling the walls to get out.

After Darius cleared away our dinner plates, I felt a soft hand on mine. It was Maggie.

"My dear," she said quietly, "you are an excellent baker. You had an off day. There's still tomorrow. Like I tell my grandkids, it's not over till it's over. You had a terrible shock this morning. Get a good night's sleep, and it will all look better in the morning."

Maggie's words were so nice, I felt like one of her grandkids.

Even Florence broke out of her giddy celebrations to say a few words of comfort. Then she got distracted when Darius walked by, his short-sleeved shirt showing off impressive muscles. She leaned in and said softly, "I do like a man who works out. Shall we ask him for dessert?"

I had to laugh. She never changed.

She took this as assent for calling Darius back over to order dessert. After making bread all day, I decided to indulge and ordered a slice of apple pie a la mode.

It arrived promptly, and I inhaled its delicious scent. I let the buttery pastry melt in my mouth until I hit the soft stewed apple. It was lightly spiced with cinnamon. Sumptuous. And a reminder of Eloise's stellar talent.

Whether I made it to the next round depended on tomorrow's showstopper. We'd been tasked with making edible bread sculptures—a total nightmare for me. I'd planned to make a flower sculpture, using some of the sketches I'd made a few weeks back when I'd had a commission for illustrations of English country gardens. The shapes of flowers was something I knew inside out. But now I was doubting myself. Was my idea going to be enough to get me through to the next round?

How was I ever going to make progress searching for my birth parents if I was booted off the show? I'd already been back in Broomewode Village two days and not made even the slightest leap forward in my quest. Instead, I'd been too busy failing to bake a tasty loaf of bread.

I'd kept an eye on the door all evening, waiting for Eloise to return so I could get my hands on that fresh yeast she promised me. But I also needed her help with getting the wow factor into my bread. Maybe she'd have some ideas as to how to take my showstopper idea to the next level.

I finished the last spoonful of pie and ice cream and sat

back in my seat, satisfied. After Eloise had treated Florence so coolly, I decided to slip away to the kitchen without explaining where I was actually going or why. I told the gang I was heading back to my room to study for tomorrow and bade them goodnight. Almost in unison, everyone told me to *actually* get an early night. I laughed. They had my number.

At the bar, Eve warned that the kitchen was super busy. "Best to come back later. You don't want to cross Sol, our chef, when he's in a bad mood. He can turn day into night with one look."

I thanked Eve for the heads-up. I knew exactly what it felt like to be hot under the collar in a kitchen—no way was I going to stride in there asking for any favors right now. Instead, I'd do what I told the others and go and study. I could come back down later when it was less busy.

Upstairs, Gateau was waiting for me, curled up in her favorite position on the armchair. I picked up one of Jonathon's bread books and slipped in beside her, pulling a plump cushion onto my lap.

The next thing I knew, Gateau was hissing and leapt off my lap. I groaned. "What is it, little one?"

She hissed again in response. I opened my eyes and looked blearily out the window. The sky was dark. I must have fallen asleep.

"Wakey, wakey, sleeping beauty."

I groaned again. "Hi, Gerry. What time is it?"

He floated over to my bedside table. "It's nearly midnight, Cinderella."

"Oh no!" I'd been asleep for hours. So much for studying. And now the kitchen was closed.

"I thought I'd give you some more advice for tomorrow."

I rubbed my eyes and said it wasn't advice I needed—it was fresh yeast and a peek inside the kitchen pantry to see what goodies I might find to spice up my showstopper tomorrow.

I stood up, stretched, and told Gerry my plan. He accompanied me downstairs, and to be honest, I was glad of the company. The inn was quiet, guests tucked away in their rooms, lights turned low. No one about but me and the resident ghost.

It was a little spooky. The pub was always so lively, so warm and welcoming. Now it was deserted. Chairs stacked on tables, the curtains drawn, lights off. No laughter or cheerful voices, no Eve behind the bar. I could just make out the hunting prints that hung on the walls, the old oak bar with its row of pumps for pulling pints of ale, wineglasses hanging upside down from hooks above them.

I pulled my cell phone from my pocket and shone a white beam of light towards the closed kitchen door. I was hit with a feeling of trepidation so strong it was tangible, like I could reach out and grab it and hold it in my hands. Why was I suddenly feeling so nervous? I wasn't doing anything wrong. Eloise had promised me some fresh yeast. But the bad feeling I'd been carrying around all day was intensifying. It felt like a clenching in the gut, a throb in my temples. I realized I was sweating.

"Gerry, I don't have a good feeling about this," I whispered. When a witch gets the death card, she should be extremely careful. And what was I doing? Creeping about in the dark with only a ghost for company. But I was pretty sure the death card was predicting the demise of my chances on the show if I couldn't pull off an amazing bake tomorrow, and for that I needed a quick midnight visit to that amazing pantry.

Gerry looked thoughtful. "Tell you what, I'll go ahead and make sure the coast is clear in the kitchen."

I didn't have time to object. Gerry disappeared through the kitchen door. The sense of unease, of unrest intensified further. It was the same feeling I got when I came across unhappy spirits, like they were weighed down by the unhappiness of their passing. He was gone for what seemed an eternity.

"Gerry?" I whispered.

He floated back from the door, a grim expression on his face.

"What is it?"

"Oh, this is not good, Poppy. Not good at all. I don't think the death card was meant for you."

"What do you mean?" My heart was beating a mile a minute.

He pointed back at the kitchen door and shook his head. "Maybe you should go back to bed. Best to stay out of the kitchen."

He was a ghost so obviously couldn't go pale, but his aspect was grim.

I began to tremble. What was happening? Was someone in danger? Was it Eve?

A sudden burst of adrenaline came over me. I ran through the door, following the beam of my phone's flashlight.

Inside the kitchen I flipped on the lights, nearly blinding myself for the moment. I blinked until I could see properly and then noticed a lone onion on the floor. I gazed at the papery yellow ball, so out of place in the pristine kitchen. Clearly, it had rolled out of the pantry.

My veins seemed filled with ice. Neither Sol nor Eloise would leave the kitchen for the night with an onion in the middle of the floor.

I glanced around for Gerry, but he was acting peculiar. Like Gateau when she was on rodent patrol in my cottage. Not that she'd ever found one inside, thank goodness, but she liked to stay on top of the situation just in case.

That's how Gerry was acting, gazing fixedly into the corner of the kitchen, then suddenly shifting. No doubt he'd tell me what he was doing at some point and in more detail than I cared to hear. But for now, I needed to check out that pantry even though every cell in my body tried to pull me in the opposite direction.

The pantry felt like a cold, black hole, the kind into which coffins get lowered. Death was in there, and I didn't need Gerry's warning to tell me that. I could feel it.

I walked forward anyway. I didn't know enough about my own talents to make assumptions. What if someone was badly injured? Would I feel that same darkness? In case that were true, I had to go forward.

Even though I didn't want to.

Gerry cocked his head and stared out the window. He was freaking me out.

Right. Quick peek in the pantry and I'd know. Standing here wasn't helping anyone. Least of all me.

I went forward, retracing the path the onion would have

taken. The door was ajar. I used my elbow to open it fully, and the light from the kitchen spilled into the storeroom onto a macabre sight.

Eloise lay flat on her back, pinned under the heavy shelving unit that had fallen on top of her. Potatoes had rolled into one corner, onions in another. Her face was covered in soft white flour like snow. Her eyes were closed, at least. I looked up. How had an entire shelf of baking products collapsed and fallen on top of her like that? Had she reached for something on an upper shelf and somehow pulled it over on herself?

With a stab of guilt, I wondered if she'd been reaching for something to help me. Raisins and nuts were scattered haphazardly all over the polished concrete floor, and spice jars had smashed, scattering their contents. The storeroom smelled of cinnamon and nutmeg and faintly of onion.

I dropped to my knees, hoping she'd only been stunned. "Eloise? Can you hear me?"

Silence.

I touched two fingers to her neck. I waited, hoping to feel the beat of her pulse beneath the skin. Blood roared in my ears. I pressed harder, desperate for a sign of life. Nothing. Her skin was cool, but that could have been from lying on cement. I was aware of a mad impulse to lay my sweater over her.

"Oh, Eloise," I said, straightening up and surveying the terrible scene before me.

CHAPTER 7

Trembling, I dialed 999. The woman on the other end of the line had a calm, steady voice. Her soft tone soothed me, and I talked her through the horrific scene in front of me. As much as I wanted to, I couldn't tear my eyes away from Eloise's lifeless body. It didn't seem right, seeing her so still. When we'd been baking, she was so animated, her hands always moving, kneading the dough or gesticulating, drawing circles in the air as she talked.

When I finished the call, Gerry came up behind me, silently shaking his head. "I can't believe it," he said. "She's gone, hasn't she?"

"Yes. I'm afraid she's dead."

He made a rude sound. "I know she's dead. *I'm dead.* But she's gone. While I'm still stuck here."

I glanced at him then. "Oh, I see what you mean." I closed my eyes and tried to feel her. I had the slightest sense of her, like the scent of perfume after a woman's left the room, faint and growing fainter. I nodded, opening my eyes. "Yes. I think she's passed over."

"And isn't that just great. She's gone, like that." He snapped his fingers, though no sound emerged. "But me? It's like there's a great party going on and I'm not on the guest list. This string of people walk right by me like I'm not standing there and slam the door behind them."

"Gerry, I really feel for you and I'm sorry, but do you think we could talk about this later?"

He threw up his hands. "Yeah. Sure. It's not like I've got anything better to do than stand about waiting. Won't be long and the next spirit will waft past me in this cursed place."

"Cursed?" I looked at him, wide-eyed. The terrible feeling that hadn't left me all day deepened, and I began to join the dots. Last week, I'd been convinced that I was a bad penny, death and destruction trailing behind me wherever I went. Elspeth, Susan and Eve had tried their best to assure me otherwise, and for a while I'd allowed myself to believe their comforting words. But just twenty-four hours after meeting me, Eloise lay dead. It didn't look like foul play—a terrible accident, perhaps. Had the shelves been loose? Too over-loaded? Had Eloise tripped, and flailing, taken a shelf down with her? I couldn't see how else such a death could happen. She must have knocked herself out. But then again, I couldn't be sure of anything these days. Maybe Gerry was on to some-thing and Broomewode was cursed. Even a simple, fun turn of the tarot deck had death staring me in the face.

"Oh, Gerry. The death card," I said, my eyes widening. "You're right. It wasn't for me. Eloise was standing right behind me when I pulled that card. Why didn't I put two and two together? Maybe if I hadn't been so obsessed with myself, I would have kept an eye on Eloise. That card was a warning, and I didn't heed it. I could have saved her, and I didn't."

"Come on. Let's get you out of here."

"I have to stay." Police would be arriving soon.

"You'll have to let them in the front door. You'll hear them better from the pub."

I let him lead the way, somewhat relieved to leave the kitchen with all its dark energy. When we got to the pub, I put on the lights. Gerry told me to sit down while I waited for the crime-scene technicians and detectives to arrive. "You need a whisky," he said. "I'd pour you one myself, but I still haven't figured out that whole gripping thing."

I smiled weakly but agreed a strong drink might help calm me. There was so much energy coursing through me, I decided to focus it. I sat at the bar and concentrated on a bottle of single malt, using the energy in my body to lift it from the shelf and set it down gently in front of me.

"You're getting good at that," Gerry said, whistling through his teeth.

"My powers are getting stronger," I admitted. "Or I'm learning how to use them."

I lifted a tumbler and brought it to rest next to the bottle. I poured myself a hefty slug of the deep amber liquid and took a sip. It warmed my throat.

Gerry could see that I was distressed and sat beside me, looking longingly at the bottle. "I could use a stiff drink, too," he said. "But it would go right through me. I wouldn't even get to taste it."

"I'm sorry." Then I recalled his odd behavior in the kitchen. "Were you looking for Eloise's spirit in the kitchen?"

"Yeah. I was hoping to catch her before she left. I thought maybe I could be her plus-one and tag along with her."

"Is it so bad? Being here?"

"I wouldn't mind if I could join you in a drink or see more than the inside of this inn and the tent, which is full of bad memories for me."

"Right." He'd suffered the indignity of being the first contestant sent home from the competition and then been murdered. No wonder he had bad feelings about that tent. "I'm sure there's a reason you're still here. Your time will come."

I didn't know how these things worked. Why some spirits passed on and others didn't. I couldn't tell him about Mildred, my kitchen ghost, who'd been in my cottage for close to two hundred years and seemed content. Then there was the soldier who patrolled outside the cottage. His appearances were sporadic, but I suspected he'd been around longer than Mildred. Would Gerry be doomed to haunt the corridors of Broomewode Inn for centuries?

I hoped not. As my powers grew more focused, perhaps I could find a way to help him. Since I had the ability to see the spirits of the departed, maybe I'd find a way to nudge them forward.

However, my first task was to help the police discover what had happened to Eloise. "Do you think Eloise accidentally pulled the shelving unit down onto herself?" I asked Gerry, hearing the lilt in my voice. I wanted him to convince me it had been an unlucky accident.

Gerry looked at me with pity. "Around here? Not bloomin' likely. Something was up with that bird. She was always moping about. Kept hanging about in the dining room. I reckon she wanted to watch the customers eat her cakes. She was insecure, like. Begging for compliments. Eve told her off, and so did that waiter who fancies himself. Adonis, is it?"

I bit back a smile. "Darius." But Adonis was pretty apropos. He was gorgeous, and he did look like he fancied himself. Not that I blamed him if women like Florence kept throwing themselves at him. "And I think she was short of money. I overheard the chef warning her that she couldn't keep getting advances on her paycheck." He'd also intimated that she might be padding her expenses, but I didn't feel like voicing that, not when her death was so recent.

If Eloise's death *wasn't* an accident, then had I witnessed anything in the last two days which might be a clue? I knew the drill by now, and the moment that DI Hembly and Sgt. Lane arrived, I was going to face the third degree. I wanted to be prepared.

I didn't have long to wait. There was a knock on the front door of the inn, locked at this late hour. I made sure to check through the window set in the door that it was actually the police standing there before I unlocked and opened it.

I'd expected a uniformed patrol to arrive first, but it was the detectives I'd come to know so well. I blinked in surprise. DI Hembly wore a tuxedo and bow tie, while Sgt. Lane wore a navy suit and a dark tie.

"Were you at a party?" I asked. I was still in shock from discovering the dead pastry chef, but seeing these two looking dressed to the nines was a second, admittedly much smaller shock.

DI Hembly said with a shrug, "My wife bought tickets to a charity event." He didn't look thrilled.

"Mrs. Hembly supports the ballet," Sgt. Lane added.

"DI Twinkle Toes," Gerry murmured in my ear.

I had to suppress a giggle, then immediately sobered when I recalled why they were here. "She's in the kitchen," I said, leading the way. I explained as concisely as I could how I'd happened to find her.

We walked by the bar and Sgt. Lane glanced at the whisky bottle and empty glass, then raised an eyebrow in my direction. "That was me," I admitted, embarrassed to be seen having a whisky at the bar. "I was pretty upset," I whispered weakly, pointing at the empty tumbler.

"No one was with you?" DI Hembly asked kindly.

"No. I didn't want to disturb anyone." I smiled in gratitude, thankful that the detective wasn't imagining that I was some kind of lush.

"All on your own?" Gerry complained loudly. "That's nice. What am I then? Chopped liver?"

I ignored the irritable ghost and led the two men into the kitchen. I'd left the lights on, and in the harsh glare, the kitchen looked perfectly undisturbed but for that single onion. In the storeroom, Eloise lay as I had found her, crushed beneath the heavy shelving unit, surrounded by broken bags of flour, tinned goods, spices and spilled produce.

I admitted that I'd knelt beside her and felt for a pulse and confirmed that I hadn't seen anyone in the vicinity.

"Why were you down here so late?" the detective asked.

"Eloise was helping me prepare for my showstopper tomorrow on the baking competition. You see, I'm not doing very well this weekend. She had some ideas on how I could spice up my final bake."

"Quite literally, I see," the sergeant said, looking down at a broken canister of ginger.

The forensics team arrived, and Sgt. Lane asked if I would step out of the kitchen with him so that they could take a statement. We walked in silence back into the dining room and took a seat at the table where just a few hours ago, I'd been trying to enjoy dinner with the other contestants. If only I'd known how bad my day was really going to get, I would have made an effort to enjoy it more.

"It just goes to show," I said, suddenly finding myself speaking out loud, "that you really don't know what's around the corner. You have to take the good as and when you can. Seize every opportunity."

Sgt. Lane looked at me in surprise. "You're absolutely right. I say almost the exact same words to myself almost every day in this job."

He smiled, and those dimples reminded me that he was a great-looking guy. Sgt. Lane looked even more handsome than usual in his tailored suit. It was sleek and perfectly cut, not the kind of thing you'd expect to see a homicide policeman rocking on a Saturday night. I suspected he'd been out on the town too. No doubt on a hot date.

"Poppy," he said gently, "let's go over your evening again. Start with the last time you saw the victim."

I nodded and began by telling him about meeting Eloise yesterday—no, wait. It was already Sunday morning. I'd said I'd met her Friday morning and how she'd been so generous with her advice. My voice wavered a bit as I talked about the dead woman. I explained all about my disastrous bread week and how Eloise had promised some fresh yeast and was going to advise me on my showstopper. "But I was so exhausted, I fell asleep after dinner. By the time I woke, it was almost midnight, and I thought I'd see if anyone was still here. I hoped she'd left the yeast out for me."

Sgt. Lane scribbled furiously in his notebook and asked if

I'd seen anyone when I came down the stairs. "Or someone leaving the inn, perhaps? Any movement in the parking lot? A car pulling away?"

Just a friendly ghost who was brave enough to go into the kitchen first.

I shook my head. "It was deserted. Kind of creepy, to be honest," I confessed. "If I hadn't been so worried about messing up tomorrow, I would never have gone into the kitchen to see if Eloise had left the yeast there for me." I paused. "Seems silly now, to be so worried about baking bread."

Sgt. Lane's warm brown eyes softened at the edges. "Don't be tough on yourself. You're working hard. You've got a goal, and that's what's important."

He had no idea. There was the ongoing search for my birth parents, my newfound powers as a water witch, the coven, my ability to see ghosts. Winning the baking competition was far from my only goal. But I swallowed it all down. It made me sad, how I had to keep things inside, hiding the things which made me *me*.

"I only met Eloise this weekend," I explained. "She was so kind. Eve told her I'd been struggling to make decent bread all week, and she let me help her prepare the weekend's dough for the inn. She shared some amazing tips." Not that I'd be able to implement them properly.

Sgt. Lane asked if she'd seemed distracted or worried. I swallowed hard when I realized that I was going to have to share what I'd overheard in the kitchen. Even though Eloise was no longer with us, it felt awful spilling all her secrets. I didn't want to betray the woman who'd helped me, but if I could make sure her death was fully investigated, then I had no choice.

"The thing is," I began, trying to choose my words carefully, "Eloise had a disagreement with the head chef. Neither of them realized I could hear their conversation—I was just out of sight by the kitchen window—but he accused Eloise of skimming money from the business." I looked down at the table. "He told her he wouldn't give her any more advances on her salary."

"Did you get any idea that she might be short of money?"

I shrugged helplessly.

"I found it hard to believe, to be honest. She seemed so up-front, so no-nonsense. But I think she was having money troubles. When she asked for an advance on her paycheck, the chef turned her down flat."

"Money's at the heart of so many disputes," he said sadly.

"She said she'd recently lost her savings. I think he felt bad for her, but the chef threatened to fire her if she didn't stop. But she countered his claim by accusing him of stealing meats out of the kitchen. He told her to mind her own business, but he sounded very angry. It was a pretty ugly dispute. But when she came back into the kitchen, she was all smiles. Like nothing happened."

"Do you know the chef's name?"

"Sol," I said. "Big guy. Tattoos. No idea of his last name."

I was about to tell him that Sol would be on breakfast duty in only a few hours when I caught movement from the corner of my eye. I turned, wondering if the murderer had come in. "Florence?" I called out.

She jumped as though walking into the inn at nearly two in the morning was normal behavior.

"Poppy! What are you doing up so late?" Then she caught sight of the sergeant. "What's going on?"

I felt like asking her the same question. Florence looked as gorgeous as always, even after such a long day. I was sure that there were bluish shadows beneath my bloodshot eyes and that my hair was a mess. But there was something different about Florence's appearance that I couldn't quite put my finger on. Was it her clothes? She was dressed in loose black trousers and a soft-looking gray cashmere cardigan, which she must have changed into after dinner. Her eyes were still heavily made up, lashes fluttering in the direction of Sgt. Lane. I realized what it was. Florence's lips were bare. She wasn't wearing lipstick. I never would have noticed this about anyone else, but it was the first time I'd seen Florence without a full pout of vermillion red or luscious strawberry pink. Combined with her slightly mussed hair, she looked much younger all of a sudden. More like the university student she actually was.

"I thought you'd gone to bed hours ago," Florence said, wagging a finger at me. But then she appeared to take stock of her surroundings, and the playfulness disappeared from her face. "Has something terrible happened?"

I turned to Sgt. Lane, desperate not to explain this latest tragedy. I was more than tired of being the bearer of bad news. He shot me a cautionary glance.

"Where were you tonight, Ms. Cinella?"

I was impressed that he remembered her so clearly, right down to her last name. He'd never remembered the burly tattooed chef. Then I clued in. Did he think Florence had anything to do with Eloise's death? No. Impossible. Still, he gazed at her, impassively waiting for her answer like a TV judge.

Her hands fluttered to her hair. "I went for a walk. Couldn't sleep. It's the pressure of this baking competition." She ran her hand over her hair, leaving a dramatic pause. Oh, and she was good at the dramatic pause the way she was good at the dramatic everything. Florence was just plain dramatic. And training to be an actress, I reminded myself.

She continued as the sergeant simply kept gazing at her. She'd had theatrical training, but he'd had training in solving crime. And interviewing suspects.

Still, he didn't think Florence could have...

Then I recalled how annoyed she'd been when Eloise wouldn't give her fresh cardamom.

But no one killed another person over cardamom.

Did they?

"DID you see anyone when you were out walking?" the sergeant continued.

She pushed her hair behind her ears. "It's the middle of the night in a sleepy village, sergeant. Who would I see?"

"Another insomniac, perhaps?"

Oh, he was good. That dry tone had her blushing. Quickly, she recovered. "I don't understand. Has someone committed a crime?" Then she came towards me. "Poppy? Were you robbed?"

I appreciated her concern, but why would anyone rob me? And of what? The most valuable thing I had with me was my cookbooks. And my cat. No one but another baker would want my cookbooks, and I trusted the other bakers. Besides, they all had their own recipe books. And no one but another witch would want my familiar. Besides, as far as I could see, all the witches in the coven had their special spirit animals.

"I'm fine," I said at last.

Sgt. Lane finally said, "The pastry chef died tonight."

Florence went pale as he spoke. "Goodness," she said, "I can't believe it. I really can't. I mean..." she trailed off.

Was Florence welling up? Surely not. Florence and Eloise had only met briefly today, and Eloise hadn't exactly endeared herself to Florence. In fact, she'd been downright rude in a way that made no sense to me.

Eve wandered in yawning, wearing a blue bathrobe and slippers. Her long hair was braided into a thick braid that hung over her shoulder.

I was so glad she was here. She must have sensed danger just like I did when I got close to the kitchen. Florence turned to Eve and blurted out the news that Eloise was dead.

Eve looked horrified. "I don't understand," she said. "I was with her just a couple of hours ago. She was strong as an ox—worked longer hours than any of us."

Sgt. Lane explained that Eloise's body had been found in the kitchen.

"The kitchen?" she repeated. "We closed up ages ago. What was she doing there?"

"That's what we're trying to find out," I said. The feeling of dread returned. Had Eloise come back to leave out the yeast for me? Was it my fault she was in the pantry so late at night? Had she been tired and knocked the shelf over? Or had she been lying there for hours? And was something more sinister going on?

DI Hembly soon joined us. He asked Eve if she could answer some questions about Eloise. She agreed but went to the bar first. The whisky and my glass were sitting there. She reached for two clean glasses and poured a couple of fingers in each. She glanced at me and held up the bottle. "Poppy?"

As much as I would've loved to drown my fears, I still had to bake tomorrow. I shook my head, and she sat down at the bar. It was strange to see her sitting at the bar instead of standing behind it, but it was pretty far down the list of strange events this evening. She took a sip and then handed the other glass to Florence. "Here, you look like you could use this. You're as pale as anything." Florence took the glass gratefully and sat beside Eve.

DI Hembly moved closer. The sergeant had his pen and notebook at the ready.

"Eloise hadn't worked here very long," Eve began, "and she mostly kept to herself. I thought she was a bit of a troubled soul. I found her crying outside by the bins on more than one occasion. But she wouldn't say what it was about. She seemed very unhappy."

"Well, she hated me instantly," Florence piped up. Then she shrugged and gave her dazzling smile. "But many women do."

"It's because you're so beautiful," Eve said. "No doubt they're jealous."

"Why would a bread baker be jealous of me?" Florence said, opening her eyes wide as though she was so far above a baker that it would be like a rock being jealous of the moon.

Sgt. Lane raised his eyebrows at me. I returned the look.

At least there was one man around who didn't fall flat at Florence's feet.

"Pops," Florence said, drawing my attention away from Sgt. Lane's wicked dimples. "You drew the death card last night, right?"

"The death card?" DI Hembly asked, looking perplexed. "Whatever do you mean?"

Eve explained that she read tarot and that she'd done a mini reading last night for a few of the baking group. Neither police officer looked impressed, struggling, I guessed, to see the significance of the story. Florence seemed not to notice and continued her train of thought. "And then you had that accident on set," she said to me. "I thought that's why you got the card. It was like a warning that you were in danger. Perhaps the shelf was meant to fall on you?"

I shuddered. Was Florence right? Was someone after me? I thought again of the tumbling rock on Susan Bentley's farm. The times I'd felt myself in danger. The warnings I'd received. Was this not about Eloise and her money troubles at all but instead about me having my fate sealed? As in coffin-sealed. I gulped.

Gerry suddenly floated over and hovered beside Sgt. Lane's notes. He shook his head, and his red spiky hair quivered.

"You guys are getting it all wrong," Gerry said. I stared at him, willing him to stop speaking. "I've been in there, examining the shelves. Not leaving fingerprints is the one good thing about being a ghost." He blew on his fingers and rubbed them on his shirt.

I glared at him and tried to follow DI Hembly and Eve's conversation. But Gerry wouldn't give up. He got right in my face. And when a ghost gets right in your face, it's literally that. "You have to make them listen to you, Pops. This was no accident. All the shelves in the pantry are bolted to the floor for safety. But the one next to poor ol' Eloise, well, guess what. No bolts. And they're nowhere to be seen. Someone must have unscrewed that shelf. Which means..."

Gerry looked at me with a grim expression.

I was following along fine. If someone had unscrewed the bolts, it would be easy enough to lie in wait until Eloise came in for something, then push the heavy shelves on top of her.

Murder.

CHAPTER 8

Gerry had proved to be the most useful ghostly sidekick. But now I was stuck with a serious dilemma. The missing bolts meant that someone had messed with those shelves. And why would anyone do that unless they meant harm? Was it possible that the intended victim wasn't Eloise? But if that was the case, then who was the intended victim? The head chef?

As I was thinking dark thoughts about the chef, Sol walked in as though I'd summoned him. With him was the gorgeous waiter, Darius. What was happening? Why was everyone up and wandering around in the wee hours?

"I saw lights on in here," Darius said, preempting the same question I was sure DI Hembly was about to ask. "What's going on?"

Hmm. That seemed a bit of an unlikely story. Had the two men been out somewhere together? I hadn't known they were friends, but then again, why would I? So much seemed to happen behind closed doors in Broomewode Village. I'd only scratched the surface in my few weeks here.

Darius hadn't been working. That was obvious. His usual uniform of black slacks and white shirt had been replaced by a white T-shirt that said Jorvik City of Vikings with two crossed axes beneath the lettering and jeans. His normally perfect hair looked tousled, like he'd been out in a strong breeze.

Sol shot him an odd glance. "My wife was coming home late from meeting up with a friend. She saw lights on in the kitchen when there shouldn't be any. She woke me, thinking there was a burglary in progress."

Eve got up with a sigh, tightening the belt on her robe. "I'll put on some tea," she said.

DI Hembly asked both men to take a seat.

"Where were you both tonight?" he asked.

"What's that got to do with you?" Sol replied.

"Stop it, Sol," Eve snapped. "Eloise is dead."

"What?" He stared at her as though she might be making it up. DI Hembly glared at Eve, but she didn't seem to notice. I was certain he'd wanted to tell the men about the death in his own way. In fact, from the way he was questioning everyone, I suspected he'd already concluded that Eloise had been murdered.

Probably the crime scene people had worked that out. All they'd have to do was look at the unbolted shelves, as Gerry had.

"The baker's dead?" Darius asked, looking at Florence as though she'd confirm it for him.

I studied them, trying to work out if they were upset for Eloise or worried about themselves—especially the chef. Sol and Eloise had a blowout—it had been all accusations and suggestions of blackmail. I wished that one of my witchy powers was mind-reading. I was sure that something juicy was crossing Sol's brain as we spoke. I could see it flicker across his eyes. The alarm deepened across his face as Sgt. Lane explained that he'd been overheard having a row with Eloise Friday morning.

Sol looked sick. He glared at Eve as though blaming her for telling the police about their argument. Then his gaze shifted to me. Oh no—did he know it was me who had overheard? He'd seen me in the kitchen all morning. Had I just angered a potential murderer?

I silently repeated a protection spell. I felt like I needed protecting. And where was Gateau when her witch was getting herself into some deep trouble?

"Yeah. We had words. Nothing important."

"How did you get on with the pastry chef?"

There was a long pause while Sgt. Lane waited for Sol to answer his question.

"All right, I suppose. Eloise was a bit of a loner," he finally said. "She arrived out of the blue looking for a job, and her cakes and bread were fantastic, so I hired her. She wasn't chatty, kept her head down and got on with the work. She's a fine baker." He stopped and corrected himself. "She was a fine baker."

There was a silence so uncomfortable, it made my toes curl.

"But she was bad-tempered and always short of money. She was on a three-month trial, but to be honest, I wasn't planning to keep her on. I suspected her of padding her budget. That's what we'd been arguing about."

"You said she turned up out of the blue. Do you know where she came from? Where her family might live?"

Sol shook his head. "I don't know. I never asked."

"You didn't ask for references?"

"Her rhubarb and ginger cake was all the reference I needed. Like I said, it was a three-month trial. If we'd made it permanent, I'd have set it up properly, done all the paperwork, but the way people come and go in this business, it's easier to try them out first."

DI Hembly turned to Darius, who stifled a yawn. "When did you last see the pastry chef?"

He threw up his arms in a gesture that was very Mediterranean somehow. "She was not a woman I noticed." He shot a glance at Florence as he said it, and louder than words he said Florence was a woman he noticed. Darius added, "She was back of house. I work front of house. We're so busy here, there's not always time to stop and chat. What I do know is that her bread and cakes were very popular with the guests. I received compliments from diners. She was good at what she did. Happy customers are good for all of us."

"It's true," Florence chimed in. "Her cakes were very delicious. Poppy and I should know—we prepare and sample mountains of the stuff. She was excellent."

I nodded. Eloise was brilliant at what she did, and yet someone had taken her life.

Why?

I glanced at Darius and noticed a slight pink tinge to his lower lip as though he'd been eating berries. I looked again at Florence's naked mouth missing its usual slick of gloss or deep berry stain. Just like after a passionate bout of kissing.

It hit me then, though I couldn't believe I'd been so slow to figure it out. Florence and Darius had been together. That's why they were both up so late.

"Do you at least know her surname?" DI Hembly asked the harassed chef.

"Her full name is Eloise Blackwell," Sol said.

DI Hembly stepped forward with a frown on his face. "You must have taken a National Insurance Number, a passport?"

Sol was a big, burly man, but in that moment, he appeared to visibly shrink into himself. Sol shrugged casually, ignoring the questions about legal paperwork. "Like I said, I tasted her cake. That was reference enough for me. If I'd planned to keep her, I'd have sorted out the paperwork, but I wasn't planning on it."

I shook my head sadly. It seemed like no one here really knew Eloise. What had made her so moody, so up and down? She'd certainly been pleasant to me and super helpful when she didn't have to be. Was she lonely and looking for a friend?

"Did Eloise live here at the inn?"

He was looking at the chef, but Eve answered.

"No. There isn't much staff accommodation. I live in as I manage the place and am called at all hours. Eloise rented a studio apartment from the blacksmith." Eve gave him Reginald's address.

Gerry floated next to me. "This is not right, not right at all." He looked so serious, so un-Gerry-like, I was worried. For once I was desperate to hear what Gerry had to say.

I asked the detectives if they needed anything else from me or if could go back upstairs. I told them I needed to rest before tomorrow's competition. They said I could go, and Florence took that as permission to leave as well, following me out.

"Poppy, I can't believe it," Florence said when we were out of earshot. "That poor woman was murdered. And she was helping you."

I wasn't sure if she was connecting those two sentences, so I sent her a sharp look, but I saw nothing but wide-eyed astonishment. "And I can't believe you were off with Darius. Shouldn't you be getting your rest for tomorrow?"

She waved her hand in the air. "I couldn't sleep, and he was handy. You know how it is."

No. I didn't know how it was. Maybe for her, men lined up dying for her attention, but it didn't happen to me. I shook my head.

"Anyway, I'm doing so well this week, I'm not too worried. Sometimes, I need to stop thinking about baking and relax." She shot me a wicked grin. "You know?"

My face did its best to respond in kind, but the reason she didn't have to worry about tomorrow was because of me. And Hamish. All she had to do was a passable effort, remember to turn her oven on, and she was set. She could afford to play with gorgeous Greeks while I had to hit the books and focus. I'd been more than happy to get some outside advice from a professional baker, but that wasn't going to happen. I had no time left to practice. And there weren't many hours left until we had to get back into the competition tent.

The only person I felt sorrier for right now was Eloise.

Gerry flapped his hands around manically. I tried to ignore him as I wished Florence a good night.

She laughed throatily. "Oh, I already had that. Good night, darling Poppy." She blew me an air kiss and was gone.

I retreated to the safety of my bedroom. Or at least I

hoped it was safe. There was nothing more unsettling than discovering a dead body, and when the cause of death was still unknown, then the whole world felt upside down.

I'd just locked my bedroom door behind me when Gerry floated through. "Jeez, you can still be polite and hold a door open for me, you know."

I apologized and asked him to spill whatever he'd been chewing on downstairs. "It looked like you had something important to tell me. You seemed very impatient all of a sudden."

"Jeez, Pops. Having only one person in the universe who can actually hear what you've got to say can make even the most patient of men go crazy—and I'm not that patient! You promised you'd work on getting me out of here. Now another spirit's flown past me. It's not fair."

"It's not a competition." But I did feel for him, and I'd been thinking about this conundrum all week when I wasn't worrying about bread. I didn't have a plan to help Gerry. "I honestly don't know. These things are kind of a mystery."

Gerry looked morose. "I feel like I'm being punished. Can't you help me move on to wherever I'm supposed to go?"

"I've never been able to help a ghost move on."

I thought about my kitchen ghost, Mildred, who'd been around for over a century, and I wondered why she'd never once asked if I could help her move on. Was it possible to truly enjoy being a spirit? Mildred certainly seemed to like pottering around the kitchen and telling me that I was doing it all wrong. If I wasn't successful with Gerry, I'd need to find ways of convincing him that haunting the inn had its merits.

"I'm going to ask Susan and Eve if they can help us," I

finally said. "Three witches are better than one. Maybe our combined powers can push you into the next world."

"You don't sound very confident."

"The truth is, I think you have unfinished business here. Only I don't know what it is."

CHAPTER 9

The next morning, I was more tired than I could ever remember being. I'd pulled an all-nighter, and I still had the most difficult day of the challenge ahead of me.

I hadn't been able to sleep more than an hour or so, and when the alarm went off, there I was, wide awake and blinking up at the ceiling. I hadn't been able to shake off the image of Eloise's body, crushed on the ground, with all the products she used every day scattered around her.

Could that be significant? Was whoever killed her sending some kind of message?

And who was Eloise, anyway? I couldn't understand why no one seemed to know anything about the pastry chef. Where she came from, where her family lived, the last place she'd worked. The lack of information haunted me. I was trying to build a picture of who this young woman was, what her life looked like, but I didn't even have the smallest detail to go on. Nothing, except that she was good at baking bread and pastry.

Hopefully when the police got to her home, they'd find letters and emails and a life full of people who cared about her and would miss her.

The alternative was so lonely.

She'd needed money for something. Maybe parents, a friend in trouble. Who knew what secrets she'd hidden? The detectives hadn't been helped by Sol not getting proper information when he hired her, and I suspected he hadn't heard the last of that. If he was investigated, what would they find out? Had he really been stealing meat, as Eloise had claimed?

I heard the cry of a hawk and ran to the window, but I didn't see the gorgeous bird. I was glad that he was around. His presence was a reminder of my quest to learn more about my father's identity. A quest that I hadn't moved forward. All night I'd been besieged by the feeling that I'd let everyone down. I'd let Elspeth down yesterday with my terrible bread; I'd let Gerry down by arriving for another weekend without a solution to help him pass over. But no one had fared worse than Eloise, who'd helped me, and now she was dead.

As if my stress level wasn't high enough, I had to bake a showstopper bread sculpture that would save my place in the competition. I felt sick to my stomach—like I'd eaten too much raw cookie dough.

I dragged myself around and woke up Gateau in the process. She'd scampered back in through the window sometime in the early hours and settled herself beside me, instantly falling asleep. It'd been a new low to be jealous of how easily she slept. Now she meowed, yawned, and stretched, and I spent a moment stroking her soft, silky fur. Just one stroke and I began to feel soothed and some of my diminished confidence began to return. Time to get up and bake. I had to give every ounce of energy to my time in the tent. Everything else could wait until filming finished. *Put your best whisk forward, Pops.*

I switched on the shower and turned the dial way up until steam began to fill the room. I stared at the mirror as it clouded over, half hoping that my mother or father would use the gushing water as a way to talk to me. A message of hope and strength in the mirror would be the tonic I needed. But nothing appeared. Not even a simple drawing of a heart in the clouded mirror, no attempt at a message that would tell me I was loved. I sighed and put myself under the water. I wanted the heat to seep into my skin, to enliven my bones. Under the pulsing water, I said Eve's protection spell once more. After Gerry's snooping had discovered that there were no missing bolts from the pantry shelves to be found on the floor, I was in no doubt that Eloise's death wasn't an accident. Someone had dismantled those shelves on purpose—which meant that right now, there was a murderer on the loose.

I dressed quickly, pulling on yesterday's slacks and replacing the blue T-shirt with an identical clean one. I ran a brush through my hair and slipped a pair of simple silver studs into my ears. Eve's amulet and Elspeth's necklace went on next, and I touched both stones, grateful for their strength.

Gateau languished in the morning sunshine streaming in through the window. I touched her little pink nose to mine. "Wish me luck, my feline friend," I said. "I'm going to need it if you want to keep enjoying these expensive bedsheets and cozy armchairs." She looked at me, bemused, and rolled onto her back, her eyes squinting in the sunlight. Nothing fazed that cat, not even the prospect of her favorite napping place disappearing. I raced out the door, keen to get down to breakfast and fuel up for the day. I was going to need a whole load of calories to get me going.

Downstairs, everyone was already eating. But the kitchen doorway behind the bar was sectioned off with police tape. And there was no cooked breakfast. Of course, there wasn't— the kitchen was out of bounds. How could I have not realized that would be the case?

Hamish waved me over and patted the empty seat next to him. In the middle of the table was a cafetiere of coffee, a pot of tea, muffins and bread with ham and hard-boiled eggs. I took a blueberry muffin and bread and an egg. "You can thank the village bakery for the baked goods, and Sol, the chef, boiled those eggs in his home kitchen and brought along the ham. Kind of him."

"It was," I said, wondering if the ham had been stolen from Broomewode Inn to start with. I poured myself a large cup of black coffee, which I needed more than anything. Maggie and Gaurav were talking bread and stopped to wish me a good morning before carrying on. Those two really were wheat fanatics—I'd never seen anyone that animated over bagels. I just couldn't get on the bread craze myself.

"You look beat, Pops," Hamish said.

That was so not the kind of comment I needed right now.

"I haven't slept," I admitted. But before I could say more, Hamish told me that he'd already heard all about last night. "Another tragedy," he said quietly. "The police are next door. They told me you found the body. I'm so sorry that happened to you. It must have been terrifying down here all alone in the dark."

All alone except for Gerry.

I nodded and asked if the police had discovered any clues

about Eloise's death or anything about her life. No one seemed to know a thing about who Eloise really was. When I thought about it, it was terribly sad.

"She was renting a room in town—" Hamish said.

"From Reginald, Susan Bentley's friend," I interrupted.

Hamish chuckled. "You're already in the know, I see. But DI Hembly discovered that she'd been paying in cash. Reginald never asked for an ID, far too trusting, if you ask me, so she could have been using a false name."

"Oh, no. But there must have been things in her room from her past? Old letters? A passport? A computer with email?" I thought about what I'd take with me if I was moving for a job, even for a few months. I'd have photos of family and friends, a computer full of the details of my life. Even my coat pockets would be crammed with notes and receipts. "Why would she use a false name? It makes no sense."

"No one's saying she did. It's a possibility, that's all. Obviously, investigators will be searching her flat for clues."

"Eloise seemed so ... " I trailed off. What did I really know about Eloise? We'd spent a couple of hours together, and although she'd been helpful, she was also jumpy and clearly in some kind of money trouble.

Hamish nodded seriously. "Why is the right question. The investigation is only beginning, but Sgt. Lane happened to see the neighbors out first thing this morning, obviously gawking to see police vehicles in the road." He grimaced. It was easy to forget that Hamish was a police officer in Scotland when we were all baking together. "One of the first things that happens when we arrive. They asked if they could help."

I bit into the pain au raisin and waited for Hamish to

finish his mouthful of pain au chocolat and elaborate. At least the pastries were delicious, buttery and heavy on the cinnamon, just how I liked it.

"But the neighbors didn't know her. They'd only waved at Eloise. They mentioned they'd seen her with a man a few times but only from afar. They couldn't identify who she was with."

"So it could have been a local or a stranger?"

"Presumably. Like I said, this is day one of what could be a long investigation."

I was perplexed. What exactly was Eloise hiding? Or was she hiding *from* someone? Had she been in danger and fled to Broomewode Village to escape, only to have the past catch up with her? I was full of questions. Hamish must have sensed my curiosity because he laid a cool hand on mine. He gestured to the police tape. "You've got a nose for trouble. A gut instinct that you should trust. But you have to put all that aside today and focus. We're both in trouble this week, and as much as I want to go on to the next round, I want to see you back here next week. No silly mistakes today, okay?"

I nodded solemnly and finished my breakfast in silence, trying to keep my mind from whirring. I was well into my second cup of coffee when Florence appeared, waved, and then joined us when she realized there was no buffet of hot food. Although she was dressed in yesterday's wonderful outfit, Florence's usual bright energy was depleted.

She looked pale, and dark shadows bloomed beneath her eyes. Was she regretting how much of her rest time she'd spent with the handsome Greek bartender and waiter? I waited for her to recite her dramatic evening—Florence wasn't exactly the most discreet of people. But she only poured herself a coffee and put an egg and ham on her plate.

"Are you excited about today?" Maggie asked her. There was no doubt that the grandmother of baking was pretty pumped. Usually Florence would gush about the competition at any opportunity, but all she said was, "I'll be glad when it's over."

Which quelled Maggie. She turned to Gaurav and rolled her eyes. He said, "I for one am anxious to get started while the weather is still cool."

He was right. The show had to go on, and it was show-stopper time. I drained my coffee and tried to focus on the task ahead. Maggie accompanied me when I went upstairs to brush my teeth. "I'm sure you'll have a better day today," she said kindly, which was sadistic if you asked me. I had nothing positive to reply to her. Not with a growing caffeine buzz and sense of impending doom. If only I could make a classic cake today and save myself with my skills. A lovely Victoria sponge, lemon drizzle, or red velvet. I'd even take on a patisserie challenge, attempt something delicate with pastry or a tricky genoise sponge. But alas. Instead, a flower sculpture constructed from bread was my destiny. I'd been counting on some magic ingredient from Eloise to aid my efforts, and instead I felt her death weighing heavy on my mind. Combine that with no sleep, the death card and a killer on the loose, and a bread garden seemed pretty unimportant.

I returned with a minty-fresh mouth and was about to leave for the tent when Edward strode into the room. He was dressed for his new role as gamekeeper on the estate. I was pleased for Edward—and only hoped he could manage to keep the shotgun-happy earl out of trouble.

Edward seemed to be looking for someone but stopped in his tracks when he spotted the police tape. He said good morning to everyone and asked what had happened. "Please don't tell me someone's been hurt."

That was a funny thing to say. If I'd walked into the inn and seen police tape, my first thought would have been that there'd been a break-in, some kind of robbery maybe.

Hamish relayed that Eloise had died in the kitchen last night. All the color drained from Edward's face. He sat down on a dining chair.

"We're not even sure Eloise is her real name," Florence said, always with the drama. "No one knows anything about her. And she looked so ordinary."

Edward ran a hand through his blond hair. "False name? Dead? But that's impossible. I saw her last night. What happened?"

"She was murdered," Florence added. If a phrase could sound like a drumroll, hers did.

Hamish glared at her. "We don't know that for certain. It's dangerous to assume foul play. You don't want to spread rumors during a police investigation." His firm voice and tough words were a chill reminder of what he did during the week.

Edward looked sick.

"You all right?" Hamish asked him.

"I'm just shocked," Edward murmured.

Poor Edward. He was taking Eloise's death so hard. Did he know her better than the others? Maybe he could help us piece together a picture of who Eloise really was. And then I wondered if Edward was the man the pastry chef's neighbors had seen her with.

But Edward had seemed sweet on Lauren, a girl from the village. He didn't seem like the type to be a two-timer, but in my experience, you never really knew with men.

I turned to him. "Did you say you saw her last night?"

Edward swallowed and seemed to stall, as if he was gathering his thoughts. Eventually, he said, "Yes. It was in the evening. We literally bumped into each other. She was in such a hurry—said she was running late to meet someone."

Hamish and I looked at each other. Could Eloise have been inadvertently hurrying into the arms of her killer?

"Do you know who she was meeting?" Hamish asked.

Edward shook his head. Of course he didn't—that would be too easy. I studied Edward's face. Like Darius last night, he looked more worried than upset. Did all the men of Broomewode Village know more about the mysterious Eloise than they were letting on?

"I'm sorry to detract from such a sorry story," Maggie said quietly, "but we're going to be late to the tent at this rate."

On our way out, we passed Darius, who looked as bleary-eyed as Florence and I. He reached out and touched Florence's arm. She paused, and Darius whispered something in her ear. She laughed but shook her head. Oh, if only I had super-hearing powers. I was absolutely dying to know what had just passed between those two. I caught Hamish watching the scene closely, too. But he only raised a brow and ushered me outside into the glorious sunshine. Even when he didn't appear to be paying attention, I suspected he was alert.

I lagged behind the group, tired and feeling entirely bent out of shape. The day was almost cruelly beautiful. The scent of honeysuckle was in the air, and the morning light was bright, already warming my tired skin. But not even the beautiful grounds of Broomewode Hall could raise my spirits. The image of Eloise's body was frozen in my mind. Yet again, someone I'd recently met had passed away in suspicious circumstances, and with the death card plaguing my mind, maybe this week was going to be the end of me entirely.

CHAPTER 10

"Is it me, or are the lights in here brighter than usual?" I said to Florence.

She tossed back her hair and laughed. "It's business as usual in the tent this morning. You're just distracted. But you've got to relax, Poppy. Else it's going to be curtains for you."

Hmm, thanks, Florence. What wonderful words of encouragement. For someone who'd had as late a night as me, and who'd been up last night talking to the police about a dead body, Florence was pretty upbeat. Also, while Gina had told me she couldn't work miracles—and what on earth had I been thinking getting so little sleep?—Florence had needed hardly any time at all in Gina's chair before appearing radiant and dewy. It wasn't fair.

I glanced at her when I should have been mentally going over the first steps of my task this morning. Did she have feelings for Darius? It was hard to believe when I'd seen her flirt with every young (and not so young) man around the village. Perhaps it was just the attention, part of what drew her to the stage—and what made her such a compelling contestant on the show. She blossomed under anyone's gaze.

And he was definitely a fine-looking man. Gerry had called him Adonis, and he wasn't far off. Still, unless Darius owned a Greek island and a shipping empire, I couldn't imagine Florence throwing herself away on him. And maybe I was being unkind. Just because she was so gorgeous herself didn't mean the poor woman couldn't also have a heart of gold.

As I set up my workstation, I couldn't help but notice that Florence kept looking out of the tent towards the visitors' area. Was she expecting someone? Maybe it was the tiredness, but I suddenly found I couldn't hold my tongue any longer.

"Looking for Darius?" I asked, putting on my best innocent face.

Oh, dear. I wasn't exactly channeling Hamish's subtlety; I was more like an electric whisk crashing into soft egg whites.

Florence widened her eyes, fluttered those thick black lashes, and then let out that deep throaty chuckle of hers—even her guilty laugh was sexy. "Oh, please. He was a bit of fun, but not someone to get serious about."

Okay, my unkind thoughts hadn't been too far off the mark. "You seemed to be pretty close last night. And again this morning."

Florence narrowed her eyes. "He's a looker, that's for sure. A great bit of fun, and he knows a thing or two about how to keep a woman happy. But Darius isn't a long-term option. I need someone who can be a solid partner, who can support me in my career and be by my side. You know what I mean?"

Hmm, I sure did. Florence wanted a man who could help

propel her into stardom, not someone who worked in a small village inn, no matter how gorgeous it was. Or how gorgeous he was, for that matter. I felt bad for Darius. Did he know how Florence wasn't taking him seriously? Although I shouldn't assume that he was serious about her either. Maybe Florence was a bit of fun for him too. I hoped so. That way no one would get hurt. Not that I'd be around to see it if I didn't smarten up and focus.

Florence leaned against my counter casually and dropped her voice even lower. "But I *am* expecting a visitor today. A real VIP."

Her cheeks flushed a pretty shade of pink, and her brown eyes sparkled. But before I could ask her any more, Fiona, the director, called for quiet.

It was time. My nerves were at an all-time high. My flower sculpture was complicated; each part was fiddly and involved some serious dough know-how. I'd only successfully put the whole lot together twice before. The rest of my practice time had given rise to burnt stalks or wilting petals.

Florence chattered on about her ideas (she was making Neapolitan ice cream cones with four different-flavored breads). It was a fun and brilliant idea, and my self-doubt bloomed, which was more than I could say for my bread flowers.

To really pull all the stops out, I was making three different types of bread—olive, pesto and pistachio—and three different flowers: rose, peony, and poppy (of course), all of which were supposed to have a beautiful green hue to look earthy and rustic. I was going to arrange them in a brown basket loaf so that they looked like they'd been freshly picked from the garden and brought inside. Well, that was the idea at least. I'd have to get through every step in the time we'd been allocated. It was going to be tight.

I arranged my ingredients in a neat row in front of me and mentally buckled in for what was going to be a seriously long day. Also a hot one, I suspected, based on how warm I already felt.

The crew zipped around making last-minute checks. I guessed they didn't want to risk a repeat episode of the light from hell crashing down to crush unsuspecting bakers—although about now, I felt like any way of escape had its merits. I'd rather be pinned to the ground by an industrial light than bake this showstopper. Oh, dear, what would Elspeth say if she knew I was feeling so negative? I closed my eyes and tried to channel her positivity, to hear her gentle voice say, *Stay calm, Poppy. You can do anything you put your mind to.*

As if the room could read my mind, the tent finally calmed down, all scurrying ceased, and Fiona called action.

Today, comedian Arty took the lead and welcomed us back to the tent. He was wearing a smart indigo shirt, and his hair had been styled to look beachy, like a surfer fresh from the waves. He appeared cool, laid-back and relaxed—my exact opposite. If only he could have lent me some of his casual savoir faire. I'd love to ride a wave all the way into the final of this competition.

Arty smiled effortlessly at the cameras and told us that today's showstopper challenge would sort the wheat from the chaff.

Everyone laughed, as we were supposed to do, but my throat was so dry, only a rasp came out. I coughed, hoped that no one had heard my ugly wheezing, and took a sip of water from the bottle on my workstation. The day was so warm, I'd need to remember to stay hydrated. I didn't want to add a fainting fit to the dough mix today.

"The judges have set you a tough task," Arty continued. "You must make beautiful, edible sculptures from bread. The emphasis here is on the word *edible*. They can't just be works of art; they need to satisfy the tummy as well as the eye."

He paused for effect and rubbed his own stomach theatrically. I was already trembling. Despite the heat, my body felt cold.

"Bakers, you have four and a half hours. And your time starts ... NOW!"

Right, Pops, no panicking. Stay cool. Stay calm. Keep your head in the game. And, technically, Arty was lying for the cameras. Bread needed time to proof, so we were due to have an early lunch break in the middle of filming. This was a lifesaver, really, because it meant I could fuel up at midday.

I tried to turn on my mental autopilot, make my hands move of their own accord. I'd made this recipe so many times at home that it should be coming naturally by now.

Tried was the operative word.

But I wasn't the only one who was distracted. In the middle of my own panic, I noticed that Florence (usually so focused) kept staring out of the tent to the visitors' area. I followed her gaze. There was no one there yet, but Edward and Sol, walked past the tent, talking seriously. I'd never seen them together before. They seemed an unlikely pairing, Edward so quiet and thoughtful, Sol more bold and confident. However, it was possible they spent tons of time together when I wasn't around. And I wouldn't have even noticed on another day. It was the timing. Eloise had only been dead for twelve hours or so, and here were two men who'd seen her on her last day talking in such a serious way.

And there was something in both their reactions to Eloise's death that surprised me. I couldn't quite put my finger on what exactly.

But what was I doing? Daydreaming about murder again when my mind had to be on bread. I snapped to attention and weighed out my ingredients. From now on, I wouldn't look up—not even to stretch my neck. Everything would be focused on my kneading techniques. I had to remember how to manipulate the dough, how to stay in control.

First up was the olive bread. Florence had given me a great tip, and I'd used her Italian supplier here in Broomewode to get some plump, juicy green olives for my bake. She claimed his sources were better than anything she could find in London. Excellent.

Ever since I was a kid, I'd loved the salty tang of green olives, and this was my favorite bread to make. I tried to recall Eloise's words, overriding the horrors of last night, and instead winding time back to when she was alive and well. I remembered that she told me not to handle the dough too much. When she observed my technique, she'd told me that I had a tendency to overwork the dough—which meant all the gas bubbles disappeared and the bread would be dense. Dense was so not the word I wanted to hear slip from the judges' mouths as they sampled my showstopper.

The olive bread recipe was simple—only five ingredients. To get through it, I just had to have a light touch and somehow turn a lump of bread dough into a peony.

I put a clean kitchen towel on a baking tray and dusted it with corn meal. I chopped my olives, resisting the urge to gobble them up. Next, I combined the flour, yeast, and salt in my mixer, and with the dough hook gently turning, added warm water until the dry ingredients began to combine. I eyeballed the mixer like I was consulting an oracle, waiting to hear my future. Was the consistency right? I was afraid of overdoing it, but was that fear going to lead me into the murky waters of not mixing it enough? Argh. I just couldn't tell. Better less than more, I figured, and switched the mixer off. I realized I'd been holding my breath and finally allowed myself to inhale deeply and exhale again.

I added my chopped olives to the dough and then took it out of the bowl and gently began forming it into a ball shape. Now for another Mediterranean trick. I coated a new bowl with a slick layer of olive oil and returned the dough to its center. I covered the lot with a clean towel and placed it into the proving drawer, where it would need to sit until it doubled in size.

Phew. One down, three to go. Now for the pistachio bread.

I finally allowed myself to look around and see what was happening in the rest of the tent. Elspeth and Arty had joined Florence, and she was as confident as ever talking through her process.

"I was raised with the idea that if you want to eat good bread, then make it yourself!" she said proudly. "Which means I've been making bread since I was about"—she paused, placed her hand down about three feet from the floor —"this high."

Elspeth laughed; Jonathon looked less impressed. Was the great Jonathon Pine about the only man in Broomewode Village immune to Florence's charms?

"I think that there's so much satisfaction when you

nurture something yourself from such simple ingredients," Florence continued, not at all flustered by the mixed reception to her anecdote. "And filling the house with the smell of bread: There's nothing better. There's a great Italian proverb I live by: *Essere buono come il pane.* It means to try to be as good as bread. Be a good person."

"Now that *is* a saying to live by," Jonathon said, looking impressed. "I could never live up to some of the breads I've eaten." Everyone chuckled. Great, not only was Florence calmer than me, she could sprout bread proverbs in Italian. I was doomed.

Elspeth asked a few more in-depth questions about Florence's flavors, and then, of course, they came to me.

"Now, Poppy," Jonathon began, "not your best day yesterday. How are you going to pull things back from the brink today?"

Oof. What a question. How charming. Thanks for reminding me, Jonathon. As if I wasn't aware of my shortcomings.

Just like Jonathon himself, I talked through the lines I'd prepared earlier again, explaining my floral arrangement, the aim for earthy, rustic flavors and colors.

"I like the idea of the basket a lot," Elspeth said softly. "It's very picturesque. But you've given yourself a lot of work to do."

Didn't I know it.

"I like some of your flavor ideas," he said. "All sounds very botanical."

I pulled together a smile that I hoped imitated confidence. "I grew up in the Pacific Northwest, which left me with an interest in nature and botany. I just feel really at peace in nature. And how could I not be inspired by the grounds of Broomewode Hall?"

I paused. Was I being convincing enough?

"The three-dimensional element looks tricky," he added.

He had no idea. "The idea is for the sculpture to look like someone has been out picking flowers from a meadow."

"Sounds lovely, Poppy," Elspeth said warmly. "Best of luck."

I was going to need it. Not even Elspeth's presence, which usually provided me with an instant, floaty kind of calm, was able to quell my worries. I felt sick to my stomach. Jonathon's words echoed in my mind as I watched the judges walk towards Gaurav. Was I trying too hard to be clever and instead courting disaster?

I glanced over at Hamish, the one who'd also struggled yesterday, though not as badly as I had. He didn't look very confident. It made me miserable to think of any of my friends going home. But it had to be one of us, and if it wasn't them ...

I put my head down and got on with the pistachio loaf. At least I could take my frustrations out on the pistachio kernels, grinding half of my batch to a fine powder. I went through the motions like a robot, trying to remember Eloise's advice without letting my brain wander off and try to figure out what happened last night. It was a real duel between Baking Poppy and Detective Poppy, and I had no idea who'd win.

Once my pistachio loaf was finished, I worked it into the shape of a rose. I reminded myself that the artistic side of things was my strong suit. My sculpture was going to be gorgeous. I slid it in to proof alongside the olive bread. Two down, two to go: a pesto focaccia and a brown whole wheat basket.

As time pushed on, I marched myself mechanically through each laborious stage of my chosen showstopper sculpture. The temperature in the tent increased with a relentlessness I found hard to bear, and I had to keep stopping to mop the sweat from my brow with a fresh kitchen cloth.

"There's another famous Italian proverb," Florence said, wiping her brow. "The loose translation is that bread made with sweat tastes better."

I had to laugh. And that made me feel less wretched.

Once my two other breads were safely in the proving drawer, I allowed myself to look around the tent again. Not that I was hoping for a bad outcome for anyone, but I was kind of downhearted to see that no one else looked as remotely stressed as I felt. My forehead had been perspiring for two hours straight, and my palms were clammy. Florence appeared cool as a clam, as did sweet Maggie and Gaurav. Only Hamish was working double quick—he seemed to be behind everyone else.

"Five minutes, bakers, until we break for lunch," Jilly called out.

I couldn't believe I had five minutes to spare. I'd actually managed to get everything done for this part of the challenge. Sadly, the hard work would really start in the second half as the bread baked and I had to arrange my sculpture.

I looked over at Florence, who had resumed her post by the side of her workstation, staring at the visitors' area, a wistful look on her face. I could just make out the profile of a tall man in a button-down shirt. Who did Florence have her eye on now?

The second filming stopped, Florence untied her apron

and fluffed up her hair. She almost ran out of the tent—I mean, as much as Florence would run rather than elegantly saunter.

I removed my own apron, thankful to rid myself of a layer and cool down. Breakfast hadn't been as robust as usual, and I needed fuel to get through the rest of the day. I followed Florence out into the fresh air.

She was already nestled next to the tall man, his arm draped around her slim body in an easy embrace. Florence was chattering a mile a minute and wouldn't have even noticed me loitering if the man hadn't acknowledged my interest with a slight bow of his head. Florence turned and beamed, waving me over.

"Poppy, come here. I want you to meet Stanley."

He extended a hand and shook mine with a firm, decisive grip. Apart from his height, Stanley had an average but pleasant appearance. His brown hair was neatly cut, and his light brown eyes were set close together but full of warmth. He was wearing a crisp white shirt and pressed trousers more suitable for a business meeting in the city than sleepy old Broomewode Village.

"Florence has been telling me all about her adventures in the tent. You've done so well to come this far," he said. If Stanley had an accent, it was undetectable. His voice was so neutral and softly spoken, I had a hard time figuring out where he was from. Who was this suave mystery man? And where had Florence found him? No, scratch that—when had Florence had the *time* to find him!

But I didn't have to wait long to find out. Almost breathlessly, Florence told me that Stanley was a film producer based in west London.

"He's come all the way up here just to see me work on camera."

If he was here on business, why did he have his arm around her? Lucky he didn't arrive last night while she was with Darius.

But I nodded and said what a pleasure it was to meet him before excusing myself to get lunch. I didn't want to linger on the idea of Florence and her many men. Maybe Darius matched Florence in the flirting department, but that's not to say his feelings wouldn't be hurt seeing her so cozy with another man.

I turned away and saw Hamish also chatting, but his conversation looked more intense. He was with DI Hembly, and I didn't think they were discussing baking.

I avoided the sandwich section of the lunch spread for obvious reasons and opted instead for some roasted red peppers stuffed with fragrant spiced rice and a large helping of Waldorf salad—a melody of apple, walnut and raisins in a lemony mayonnaise dressing.

I was about to take a seat and eat my lunch when I caught sight of Edward striding along the path in the direction of the inn. He looked so upset that I put down my longed-for plate and was about to investigate whatever was plaguing my friend when I felt a hand on my shoulder.

It was Hamish. "Don't," he said quietly but with such an edge to his voice, a chill went down my spine. "Give Edward a wide berth."

Hamish's broad brow was furrowed, and despite the afternoon heat and all the intensive work in the tent, he looked cool and focused.

"Why should I avoid Edward?"

"Eloise's neighbors identified Edward as the man they saw visiting her from time to time. Which means, Poppy, he's their prime suspect. What's more, Sol told Sgt. Lane that the roast Eloise saw him take was actually for Edward—he cooked her dinner in his cottage the night she was killed."

I stared at Hamish, wide-eyed. Kind, gentle Edward? The creative gardener with green fingers? The man who was helping Lauren the bride to overcome her grief after the murder of her husband-to-be—who perhaps meant more to her than her cheating ex ever had? I couldn't understand it. If Edward and Eloise were friends, or even lovers, why would he kill her? And why would he lie about bumping into her the night she died if she'd been at his cottage eating dinner?

CHAPTER 11

*A*ll too soon I was back in the tent, standing at my workstation like a statue. Even after Hamish coached me, telling me that nothing was confirmed yet and things weren't always as they appeared in murder cases, I couldn't get over that Edward was the prime suspect in Eloise's murder investigation.

Robbie, the sound guy, attached my mic pack. "You okay?" he asked. "You seem distracted."

Oh, man. He was right. I was distracted, and I was going to have to fix that.

I smiled weakly and told him that I was worried about the showstopper. It had to be a knockout, otherwise I was getting knocked straight out of this competition.

"You're still the favorite," Robbie whispered, a sly grin on his face. "The crew's got some bets going on who'll win." He leaned in. "I've got twenty quid on you. Don't screw up."

I cheered up immediately. Talk about putting your money where your mouth was. Then my stomach dropped. What if I lost? Then everyone in the crew who'd believed in me would lose money. I knew it was just for fun, like their poker games and the silly jokes they played on each other, but my stress level went up another notch.

"I hope you can afford to lose your twenty."

"Everyone is allowed one bad day. You can pull it back. Just keep your head in the game."

Huh. I'd heard that one before. As if it was that easy when (a) you couldn't make delicious bread for the life of you, and (b) you were caught up in a murder investigation and couldn't banish its details from your mind.

"Chin up," Robbie said. "It's going to be okay."

I retied my apron and gave him a confident smile. If I couldn't be confident for real, then I'd have to fake it to make it.

The countdown was on. In five minutes, I'd have to finish this whopper of a showstopper. I wasn't even allowed to pull out the proving drawer yet to see if the dough had sufficiently risen. What was it that Eloise said? Not to let too many gas bubbles disappear. Argh. I couldn't remember it all.

Suddenly it was all happening again. Sound: check. Lights: check. The cameras were poised and waiting. Fiona called action. It was showtime.

I opened the proving drawer with my breath held.

Phew. All four breads looked like they'd risen properly. I carefully slid them from their resting place and got ready to work that dough.

The problem was, my hands were shaking. "Calm down," I whispered to my palms. "Pull yourselves together. You're letting down the team."

The bread basket was the shape that worried me most.

During my endless hours of practice, it had either worked brilliantly or collapsed or burned to a brittle mess and then broken. I figured my chances were even. The idea was to shape the basket over an inverted bowl that had been covered with aluminum foil and bake it bowl and all. I'd begun with the wrong-shaped bowls—either too shallow or too deep or not wide enough. Now I had the perfect size, but timing was everything. The basket browned so quickly on the top, it was difficult to avoid that *and* ensure the rest of the dough was cooked through. It looked simple enough when it was done right, but it was a nightmare to get everything perfect.

I buttered the bowl and floured it lightly. I floured my workstation and rolled the dough into a large rectangle. With a pizza cutter, I divided the dough into quarter-inch strips. Now for the fiddly bit. I took one strip, rolled it back and forth until it became rope-shaped. So far, so good. Six more ropes to make. I wiped the sweat from my temple.

Once these were done, I laid the strips from one end of the bowl to the other, weaving the ropes into a basket until the entire bowl was covered. Quickly, I snipped off the excess, brushed the lot with egg wash, and took it over to the oven to bake until it was golden brown. I wished it well, of course, but I had a feeling I'd need a lot more than my well-wishes for this beast to bake into a beauty.

Now for the remaining parts. I traced the top of the bowl on parchment paper and made three more dough ropes into a braid to fit the circle for a lovely decorative top (I hoped) and then another braid to make the handle. These went into the oven for fifteen minutes, and if I had my calculations right, all three parts would come out at the same time.

I was still sweating, my breath labored and heavy. There

was still so much to do. I stared down the three remaining doughs, each such a gorgeous shade of green I almost—almost—forgave them for being my nemesis.

Of course, this is when Arty decided to see how I was doing.

He breezed over in his trendy outfit and asked me to explain my process for kneading the dough and shaping them into three different flowers. To be honest, I was feeling so unsure of myself, I would have loved to ask the same question, too. Could I phone a friend? Ask the audience for help?

I cleared my throat. "It's been a lot of trial and error with this one," I confessed. "As we already know, bread is not my strong suit. I'm trying to make up for it with flavor and a little pizzazz. And what I do know is flowers. I've read a lot of botanical books and filled sketchbooks of my own. I'm hoping that expertise will transform this dough into something special."

"How's your timing looking? You've got a lot to get through."

Oh, great. Had Arty decided to be the new Jonathon Pine and give me a hard time? The more I had to explain to this wise guy, the less time I had to actually bake. These little filming asides were torture when you were under pressure.

"All I can do is my best," I told him, trying to convey the same message to myself.

Thankfully, Arty wished me good luck and moved on to Florence. He was probably desperate to speak to someone not sweating profusely with a look of pure panic welded to their face.

I listened as Florence chattered, her pretty laugh tinkling.

How I envied her cool, calm delivery. Her ability to multitask. And then I made the massive mistake of stopping momentarily to look around the tent. A mistake because everyone seemed so focused and in control. Maggie was making an enormous Ferris wheel, and so far it was seriously impressive, sure to be much bigger than anything else the group produced. Each spoke of the wheel alternated flavors, some cheese, some seeded, some with nuts baked in. I was in awe of Maggie's know-how. As I followed the progress of her showstopper from afar, the feeling of gloom I'd been fighting so hard to stave off returned. It spread through me as easily as butter on warm toast. What was even the point of it all? I had zero chance of pulling myself through this round.

As if she had sensed my sadness and sprung into action, Elspeth suddenly appeared by my side. She did not say a word, simply smiled that lovely smile of hers. So warm. So encouraging. And my doom began to dissipate. Finally, she said, "Looking lovely, Poppy. Perhaps time to check the ovens," and disappeared as quickly as she came like the perennial fairy witch mother she was.

The ovens! I snapped back into life and dashed over to where my basket would surely be overcooked.

I opened the door with trepidation, feeling the lens of the camera watching over my every move. I let out my breath. Okay, the basket was a little crisp around the edges but definitely not burned. I took my bread wares back to my workstation and set them aside to cool while I continued with my flower shapes. They didn't take so long to cook, so I had time to get each one right. Or so I hoped.

I worked with my head down, once more trying to

channel Eloise's energy into my fingertips without bringing to mind the image of her dead body. Not easy.

I mixed ingredients and lovingly shaped my flowers, twisting and braiding and manipulating the dough. I made fresh pesto, which filled my workstation with the delicious scent of basil and pine nuts and would hopefully turn into a piquant and tasty filling to one of my flowers. I did everything I'd set out to do, not one silly mistake. It was like my hands were following a well-worn path, not thinking, just moving, and my brain was a separate thing, whirring away, distracted and yet somehow still managing to process what my body was doing.

I sent my flowers into the ovens, wishing them well, and returned to the workstation to assemble my now-cool bread basket with toothpicks.

It was a delicate job. I needed the basket to be sturdy enough to hold the bread flowers, but I didn't want to pin the pieces together too tightly for fear of the basket crumbling. I was unsure of myself and spent far too long dithering, umming and erring until I captured the amused attention of Jilly.

"Think whipping out a tablecloth from under a laid table," she suggested, miming the action like an old-fashioned pantomime. "Be quick like a cat. Time's a-tickin.'"

But I barely cracked a smile. It was all fun and games to these comedians, but right now I was deadly serious.

I managed to pin the bread basket together without breaking anything. The braided ring around the top was definitely overdone, but all I could do was hope that they ate a bit of the handle instead. Argh. It was torture thinking that within the hour, all this hard work would be destroyed and fill the bellies of cast and crew.

I went back to the ovens to check on my bread flowers. They needed a little more time, but I couldn't bear to leave them alone, so I looked longingly into the depths of the oven, trying to transmit well wishes and good vibes for a successful rise.

And who joined me in my oven vigil but Gerry.

"Yeesh, these ovens still give me heebie-jeebies," he said, shaking his head. "I reckon I ended up crisper than your burned pastry. That'll teach me to mess with married women."

I sighed. I so did not have time for a trip down memory lane with Gerry. As much as I wanted to completely ignore Gerry's presence, something he said struck a nerve. Gerry had been murdered over his affairs with married women, and there was something about Florence's new squeeze that I couldn't quite put my finger on. He seemed ... well, married. Was I being crazy? It was a strange hunch, but there was just something in the way he carried himself that gave the impression he belonged to someone else. And I wouldn't put it past Florence to know that he was married and carry on regardless. She was an epic flirt, and it seemed like he would be good for her career. Not that I thought Florence was that callous—it was probably more of a subconscious thing—but an aspiring actress dating a film producer? Now that *was* a marriage made in heaven.

Thankfully my attention was brought back by a dinging timer, and I removed my flowers from the oven. To my relief, they appeared to be fine—not undercooked, not burned. But that didn't mean I was out of the woods yet. It still had to taste good!

Before I knew it, Jilly was calling time. I'd managed to arrange everything in my basket, and the finished sculpture was pretty—the greens and browns rustic and lovely, just as I'd hoped. The only thing letting Team Poppy down was the basket, which against the baked flowers was clearly over-cooked. But I was hoping that the judges might figure that if it all tasted good—which was a big *if,* considering my track record—then that little oversight could be forgiven.

I added my showstopper to the judging table, and my heart sank. The row of other showstoppers displayed one wonder after another. An array of curious and fantastical sculptures, so varied and imaginative. I was super proud of all my friends even as I wondered if my sculpture could stack up.

There was Florence's Neapolitan ice cream bonanza, Hamish's Shetland pony, Maggie's Ferris wheel and Gaurav's bicycle. And then my bread garden. The runt of the litter. Overcooked and not anywhere near as ambitious as the others, even though I'd tried my best to get out of my comfort zone and create something spectacular.

I took a deep breath. Out of the corner of my eye, I saw Gerry float back into the tent and stand next to the table of showstoppers. He spotted mine, looked pleasantly surprised, and gave me two thumbs-up. Then changed his mind and put down one thumb. Thanks, Gerry. But he hadn't actually tasted the thing.

Was there even any point in listening to the judging? It was going to be pure heartache.

First up was Florence.

"I think what you've produced there is a work of art,"

Jonathon said, shaking his head in wonder. "It's actually making me salivate just looking at it."

"Agreed," Elspeth said. "The colors and arrangement are sumptuous. I can imagine I'm eating gelato on the Amalfi coast. But"—Elspeth paused for effect—"the perennial question is whether it tastes as good as it looks."

I watched as Elspeth tore off different parts of Florence's ice-cream-shaped extravaganza. Murmurs of "delicious" and "nice balance of flavors" echoed around me.

I was next. My mouth was dry, but my forehead was perspiring. *So* not a great combination. And on top of all that, I was trying not to twitch with nerves. I forced myself to relax my hands and straighten my spine. I knew one camera was trained on me, ready for my reaction, while two others captured the judges.

As Elspeth commented on the beautiful color of my flowers, I couldn't help but feel she was buttering me up with compliments before she was going to have to deal the heavy blows. Even Jonathon was being kind, highlighting my braiding work on the breadbasket, but eventually he had to concede it looked a little crispy.

I watched with eyes half-closed as they sliced through my creation and then chewed.

"Although lovely looking," Elspeth said, "this peony is a little flat. I think the dough's been overworked."

To my dismay, Jonathon agreed, and proceeded to tear off pieces of bread from the other flowers.

"The flavors are lovely," Elspeth said. "Good combinations which show that a lot of thought has gone into this showstopper. But the texture of the bread isn't wowing me,

I'm afraid. It's underworked in parts and overworked in others. And the basket is a little on the crisp side."

"A nice-looking sculpture," Jonathon added, "but lacking the refinement of a master baker."

Wow. I felt like Jonathon had reached across the tent and scooped out my heart with a tablespoon. *Lacking refinement.* The sad thing was, I couldn't even argue differently. The judges were right, although Elspeth had wrapped her feedback in a kinder bow. It was wrong of me to feel so betrayed, but Jonathon was a fellow witch, after all. Couldn't he be, well, a bit nicer? Receiving critiques like that felt so personal, even if they weren't meant to be delivered that way.

But the judges had lost interest in me and already moved on. I barely registered what either judge said to Gaurav, but by the shy look of pride on his face, it was good.

Hamish was next. He'd had difficulty this week just like me, but the judge's comments were peppered with the kinds of adjectives any baker would want to hear. His Shetland pony did look very messy (it was undeniable), but the judges forgave him because his bread was airy, light and flavorful. I might have scored some marks on the aesthetic front, but where it really counted, I hadn't been able to step up to the mark.

Last was Maggie. I'd put a million bucks on hers being the best of the bunch.

"Maggie, in terms of texture, this is leaps and bounds ahead of the others," Elspeth said.

Maggie beamed. "My grandchildren's favorite," she replied. And then, more softly, "Thank you so much." She was so humble and always looked surprised when the judges praised her work.

The judges went to confer and decide on today's winner as well as who'd be going home. I knew my sculpture wasn't perfect, but Hamish had received some harsh words about his Shetland pony looking more like a sad donkey. There wasn't a single part of me that wanted Hamish to return home this week for good. I wanted him to stay and excel—to go on and win this thing! He deserved it. But this was the rap with the competition. Now that I knew and adored each and every one of my competitors, how could I wish the worst for them? I wanted us all to go through. Why couldn't we all just stay put and bake our little hearts out?

I caught Hamish staring at me and knew he was thinking the same thoughts I was. I reached out and gripped his hand. "Whatever happens, we did our best."

I stood in place, silently hoping for a bread miracle, that the judges couldn't decide and so put us all through to the next round.

When Elspeth and Jonathon returned, I couldn't read either of their faces. Were they sad that one of us was about to go home? I tried my best to emulate their neutrality. I was schooling myself not to cry. I wanted to ride the wave and be grateful for the journey I'd been on so far.

"Bakers," Elspeth began, "to come this far in the competition, you've all had to show mighty grit, determination, and above all—talent."

"There was a standout baker today, and that was Maggie," Elspeth said, turning to face Maggie, who was a delightful shade of pink. "Without doubt, you are our Star Baker this week."

Jonathon complimented Maggie again. "Today you baked The Best Bread in Broomewode."

A round of applause rippled through the tent, and I followed suit. But my brain was working overtime. Best Bread in Broomewode? A flash of Friday's conversation entered my head. What was it Eloise had said? Be the best at what you do. And then she'd mentioned the best turf cakes in York. How could I have forgotten that detail? Was it a clue to where the mysterious baker came from?

CHAPTER 12

"But of course, this part of the day isn't all celebration," Jonathon continued.

No. It wasn't. It was about impending doom and heartache. Was I being paranoid, or could I feel everyone's eyes on me, waiting for the terrible news, watching to see how I'd react?

I kept my eyes glued straight ahead. *Stay cool, Poppy. Don't embarrass yourself with an outburst of emotion.*

"Having to say goodbye to someone each week gets harder and harder as we go on," Jonathon continued. "And without a doubt, the person that we're saying goodbye to this week is a fantastic baker, full of creativity. A real strong contender. It's someone that we've all enjoyed having in the tent, and I know they're going to be missed."

There was a long pause. It was pure agony.

Elspeth stepped forward. "So it's with sadness that I have to say that today Poppy will be leaving the tent."

EVEN THOUGH I'D expected to hear my name, I was still caught by surprise. From beside me, Florence pulled me in for a hug, and before I knew it, the whole group enveloped me in a massive bear hug. And just like my brain and body had separated while I was baking earlier, I felt myself float up and watch the scene as if it was happening to someone else.

For so many weeks, this had been my ultimate fear. My whole reason for coming on to the show was to find out about my birth parents. I'd been determined to stick around in Broomewode Village for as long as it took. However, I'd come to love the competition, to look forward to another week creating baked goods under the harsh eyes of two judges, two comedians and eventually millions of home viewers around the world. And now here I was, leaving the tent for good. By all rights, I should be devastated. But instead, a massive wave of relief flooded through me. I realized that I was proud of myself! I didn't think I'd have it in me to get this far. I'd taught myself how to bake and pushed my skills further than I thought they'd ever go. I'd exhausted myself in the process. But I did know that I'd gotten better. Much better. Not bread week good, but good enough to get to week six. And that was enough for me.

I was brought back down to earth by the sound of crying.

"Florence," I said, turning to her in surprise. "Don't cry!"

She let out a sad sob. "But you're my best friend here. How am I going to do this without you?"

"Ditto." It was Gerry. "I need you here, Pops. You can't leave Broomewode Village. Who will I talk to? I don't want to spend my days scaring the guests at the inn. It's so lonely. And boring. I'm bored of out my mind here."

He looked so forlorn, it was like I'd been sucker-punched in the stomach. I wanted to tell him that I hadn't forgotten my promise. I was going to help him pass over to the other side.

Before I even had time to pretend I wasn't listening to a ghost, Fiona rushed me outside to record my exit interview.

My exit interview. I'd watched the other contestants film theirs, never once thinking about what my parting words would be. I should have prepared for this moment. Shame I was too busy burning bread to think about it properly.

The sun hit me with its full force as I followed the camera and sound men. I welcomed the fresh air, taking deep lung-fuls. The tension eased in my body. I didn't have to worry about bread anymore. Or cameras following my every move as I sweated it out in the tent. It was a simple joy but one I felt so deeply.

"Here's good," the cameraman said, pointing to a spot by the side of the great tent. A great oak was on my left, its leafy branches swaying gently in the afternoon breeze. I waited as the rest of the crew set up the shot and let my eyes travel over the vista before me. In the distance, Broomewode Hall glowed golden just like the first time I'd set eyes on its glorious turrets and lead-lined windows. But today it looked less imposing and more familiar. It was weird, but the great hall had something of a homely feel about it now.

I let my eyes wander farther. Abundant flowerbeds, meticulously groomed lawns, the ornamental lake—it was so beautiful. I didn't want to start welling up. A runny nose and puffy eyes in front of millions of viewers? No, thanks. This was the last time I was going to need to hold it down and be strong for the cameras. I wasn't about to let it all hang out now.

I pulled myself together and braced myself for the emotional questions I knew were heading my way. I wished they'd given me a minute to go and see Gina, have a hug and a makeup refresh. I'd barely slept, spent hours in that hot, sweaty tent, and now I had to face the cameras and put a brave face on my defeat. I just hoped that my exhausted face didn't scare the viewers.

But just as I'd resigned myself to looking my worst, I saw Gina running over from the tent, waving a lip gloss in her hand. "Stop, stop!" she called out. "Don't you dare begin filming without me."

I laughed, so pleased to see my best friend. She stopped in front of me and took my face in her palms. "You were amazing," she said quietly but firmly. "Amazing. I can't wait to sit down with a Chinese takeaway and tell you how proud I am of you. But first things first. Let's fix this face."

Gina pulled out a compact powder and bronzer and got to work on my face. I closed my eyes and let her do her thing. Gina always knew how to get the best out of my features.

A minute later, she whispered that she was done and stood back. "Perfect."

I grasped her hands and thanked her for having my back. Or my face, I should say.

The camera team cleared their throats very loudly. Gina spun round and good-naturedly told them off. "Okay, okay, I'm leaving!" She laughed.

The camera started rolling, and one of the assistant producers locked eyes with me. "How are you feeling, Poppy?"

I took a breath. Here it was. My final segment on *The Great British Baking Contest*. "In a way, it's a massive relief.

You're under so much pressure in the tent, and I knew this week I'd reach the limit of my abilities. I knew bread week would be my weakest, and it was."

I stopped and laughed at myself.

"But I'm gutted, of course. I don't want to say goodbye to everyone. Getting to spend time with the other bakers every weekend has been incredible. I've made some amazing friends here. Friends for life. They've taught me so much."

I paused for a moment, reflecting on all the friendships I'd made both in and out of the tent. A whole witches' coven. I was so lucky to have so many wonderful people in my life. How could I feel sad?

"The other bakers have become like family, really," I continued. "They're so supportive and encouraging. We all rally round each other. I'm adopted, and so the idea of family is so important to me. I'm so lucky to have found my people."

I swallowed. I hadn't meant to get so personal. *Do not well up, Poppy.* But despite myself, I felt tears prick my eyes.

The cameras cut and the crew thanked me, saying it was a perfect exit speech. "The audience will eat it up," Fiona added, who'd been watching from afar.

"More happily than my bread sculpture, I'm sure," I joked.

I thanked everyone and was about to return to the tent to clear up my seriously messy workstation when I saw Elspeth waiting by the lake.

I excused myself and said I'd be right back.

At the sight of the great Elspeth Peach, baking judge extraordinaire and self-appointed fairy witch mother, my heart sank. I felt like I'd let her down.

Despite the heat, Elspeth looked as cool and calm as ever.

She gave me a sad smile as I approached and reached out with both her hands to grasp mine. The jolt of electricity that shot through my arms was stronger than ever. I remembered when I'd feared that jolt. Now it was calming, reassuring. A link to my sisterhood.

"You lasted a very respectable amount of time," Elspeth softly.

I nodded. "Longer than I'd even hoped. I'm sort of proud of myself, really."

"Take comfort, Poppy dear. You couldn't win, not being a witch and with Jonathon and me being watched so carefully by the Witches' Council. But you did very well to come this far."

I was so shocked, my mouth fell open. Had my bread not been as bad as I'd thought? "Wait, Elspeth. What are you saying? Did you ruin my bread by magic?"

Elspeth laughed. "No, dear. I'm afraid you managed to ruin it all on your own."

Oh. Great.

"But I'm very sorry to see you go. Once we realized you were a witch, we couldn't let you win. However, Jonathon and I agreed not to interfere until we had to. If you'd made it to the final round, we'd have sadly chosen the non-magic contestant over you."

It made sense, but since I wasn't using magic in my baking, it would have felt unfair. I bet the witch judges were relieved they hadn't been forced to make that choice. Lucky for all of us, I'd failed all on my own. No, I reminded myself. Not failed. I'd worked my butt off and come further than I'd believed.

I was calling that a win.

"I hope you'll visit Broomewode Village now that you have friends here and continue your search for your birth parents."

"Yes," I said resolutely. "I think my focus wavered. I was trying so hard to stay in the competition. Now I can put all my energy into my search. I know so much more than I did a few weeks ago. It's time to join the dots and get back on the trail."

Elspeth hugged me and told me to keep in touch. "You're part of the coven, Poppy, which means you're never alone. Your sisters are always here for you. You never know when you'll need us."

Even though I'd been booted off the show, I felt like the luckiest witch in the world with a woman like Elspeth Peach looking over me.

I walked back to the tent with a spring in my step. I had a clear plan. See if Eve and Susan could help with the Gerry problem, get back on track with the search for my dad, and speak to DI Hembly and Sgt. Lane about Eloise's comment. If York *was* her hometown, then it could really help the investigation.

It wasn't until I was saying goodbye to all the crew that Elspeth's words echoed in my ears: *with Jonathon and me being watched so carefully by the Witches' Council.* What on earth did she mean?

CHAPTER 13

*L*eaving the tent for the final time, I tried to hold on to the feeling of lightness that had come over me when I was voted off the show. But hearing that the ruling body of witches was watching Elspeth had re-opened my curiosity about my role in the coven and how my birth parents fitted into the picture. It was like the questions that had been plaguing me last week were suddenly allowed to fly into my head now that I was no longer trying to keep my place in the competition.

And as my mind began to wander, I tuned out of the chatter of the group as they made their way back to the inn. Something Eloise had said to me on Friday reentered my brain. She'd been talking about being the best at baking and becoming renowned for one type of cake and had mentioned making the local papers. The local papers—why hadn't I thought about looking at the archives for an obituary that might help me find my dad? I hadn't had time last week to follow up on Gerry's suggestion to find a record of deaths in the area in the last twenty-five years since I was born. But now was the time. Gerry was right: How many young men could have died around here in any given year? Or perhaps he wasn't so young. It was hard to tell with a ghost. But I was counting on there not being too many men in the area who'd died in the last twenty-five years while in the prime of life. Surely I'd be able to narrow it down?

I needed to know what had happened to my dad. I knew that he'd been pretty young when he died. And I felt in my gut that he was a local man, not someone visiting, despite what Katie Donegal had told me about my mom taking trips to London on weekends. His ghost was in Broomewode Village, and it was here for a reason—more than to pop up every so often to warn me to get away from this place.

So I did a Poppy special: told the others I needed some alone time to process what had happened today. "I'll join you in the pub in an hour or so."

I could see that Florence was about to protest, but Maggie put a hand on her shoulder, shaking her head. "It's been an emotional rollercoaster for all of us this week. The least we can give Poppy is some time to herself," Maggie said.

"Just stay safe," Gaurav added. "We know what happens when you wander off."

I promised everyone I'd keep my phone on ring and be with them soon. "And you can have a glass of fizz waiting for me."

"A bottle, darling," Florence promised.

I turned away from the group and took out my phone. A quick search online led me straight to the local newspaper archives. It looked to be a tiny building next to Broomewode library, a few streets away from the Italian deli and grocer. The answer to the mystery of my dad's identity could have been here all along, right under my nose. I cursed myself for not thinking of it sooner. I'd been too caught up in the competition.

With Broomewode Hall in the distance behind me, I made my way into the center of the village, the streets cobblestone now, soon reaching the rows of charming houses and little shops with flats above. There was the charity shop where I'd once coveted a crockery set but never had the time (or spare cash) to return and purchase it; the deli where Florence bought her chestnut flour; a butchery; the post office; Reginald's Broomewode Smithy. A new thrill raced through me. Soon I'd have more time to explore this community. I loved Norton St. Philip, but there was a special (well, let's face it—magical) something about Broomewode Village. There was so much more to this village than I'd even begun to uncover. Each new walk through its grounds brought a new discovery. It was like the place held me in an embrace, everything cast in a golden haze, the air always clean and filled with the perfume of blossoms. I wanted to return to the woods and explore the land around the stone circle. I'd always loved forests as a child. The alive, mossy scent, the rough texture of old bark, pine needles beneath my feet and all the little creatures scurrying across the earth, over fallen branches and crisp leaves. Being in nature was an endless joy to me and an inspiration for my baking *and* my design work.

Then there were the lakes and streams where I'd seen visions. I was a water witch, so it made sense that I'd be drawn to my element.

Of course, I'd have to work again soon. My bank balance was worryingly low after so many weeks buying baking produce and turning down graphic design work in favor of slaving over my electric mixer. But reality could wait till next week. For now, I allowed myself to be immersed in the beauty of the village, the rows of hanging baskets bountiful with bright blossoms, the sounds of the birds chirping and the faraway shrieks of kids playing in the playground. A gentle breeze softened the rays of the sun, and for a moment, I felt peaceful. Peaceful but determined.

I checked my phone again and took a left turn. The newspaper office was tucked behind the main street. I saw the library first. A small building with a grand attitude, the library was built from the same golden Somerset stone I'd come to recognize around these parts, but its entrance was embellished with two colonnades, above which gold letters read "Public Library." I would have loved to slip between its doors and browse the shelves, but that luxury would have to wait. It was the library's little neighbor that was my destination.

Broomewode News had a far less fancy front and was clearly a repurposed cottage. It wasn't very impressive to look at, but I knew better than anyone that it was what's inside that counts. Although there wouldn't be any cream cheese frosting or sweet jam inside, this innocuous structure could help unlock the secrets of my past.

I walked through the doors, my excitement rising. Was it possible that I was just a few steps away from discovering my birth dad's identity? There was a bored-looking woman sitting at a desk who glanced up when I entered. "Can I help you?"

"I wonder if I could look at your archives," I said.

"Whatever for?"

She looked as though it was a very strange request. Why

had I not prepared a story? I couldn't tell this woman I was hoping to find my father in dusty old files. I was trying to think of something to say when a chubby man with curly red hair and a beard walked in the front door. He looked as hot as I'd felt in the tent. His short-sleeved shirt was creased and bore sweat rings under the arms. His face was the color of a ripe apple. I'd seen him at the initial press events in the village. He was a reporter. He glanced at me, then did a double take. I hoped he'd keep walking but he stopped. "You're one of the bakers," he said.

No point denying it. I nodded.

"We're not allowed to report on the progress, but hard luck. I heard you got voted off today."

No point denying that, either. "Thanks."

His eyes began to sharpen. "You here to give us a scoop? Dark secrets in the competition tent?" He seemed to be joking but also not. Like he doubted I was here to unfold some juicy story but remained hopeful.

I immediately told him I was here on a private matter.

"She wants to search the archives."

"Whatever for?" he asked.

Now that I'd had that couple of minutes, I felt more prepared. "Obituaries," I said in what I hoped was a casual way. "I think I had family from around here."

His eyes narrowed again. "I thought you were adopted." He might be a reporter in a small town, but he was sharp. He must have read all the bios of all the contestants and remembered them. Impressive.

"I am. My adoptive mother had a cousin who lived here. I promised I'd search for information about him while I was here, and now I have time. Unfortunately."

"Do you know when he died?"

Oh, this was getting messy already. "I'm not exactly sure. I have a range of dates."

He shook his head. "This isn't the British Library. Anything older than ten years is on microfiche, and we need to know what year and date to pull the right paper. The old issues are in file drawers and boxes. You have to make an appointment."

"I couldn't have a quick look now? I'm leaving tomorrow."

He and the woman behind the desk exchanged a glance. "You'll be here hours. There's no quick look when you go through old microfiche."

That was disappointing, but then I was so tired right now, and I didn't want to keep the rest of the contestants waiting. What if they thought I was a sore loser? I supposed I could make an appointment and return when I felt fresh.

"Wait," the woman behind the desk said. "What about Mavis?"

I turned back. "Mavis?"

The reporter nodded. "Mavis. She's like human microfiche. She's been here since King Arthur reigned. Knows most everyone. Writes the obits. She might remember your mother's cousin. It's always possible."

I was so grateful, I wanted to hug him, sweat stains and all. "She works on a Sunday?"

"We're open seven days a week. We all take different days off. In theory, it works. In practice, I never seem to have a day off. I'm the reporter, editor and photographer, with help from a few stringers. Mavis is what we call the inside editor. She runs the newsroom, takes all the calls, writes a garden column and the obits."

The other woman glanced at her watch. "She'll be leaving soon. You'd better hurry if you want to catch her."

"I'm Trim, by the way," he said, putting out a hand.

"Trim?" Seemed a cruel nickname for someone on the weightier side.

"Theodore Trimble. Trim stuck."

"Okay. Hi, Trim. I'm Poppy."

"Good to meet you. Let's see if Mavis has time for you."

I followed him up a set of stairs. He said, too casually, "I've just come from Broomewode Inn. Had a mysterious death, I understand. You're staying there. What'd you see?"

Oh, no. I wasn't falling for that. The last thing the police would want would be someone like me giving away the details of the investigation. I gave him my blandest look, and I can be very bland when called upon. "I know the names of the detectives on the case. I could give them to you if you like."

His face broke out into a boyish grin. "Can't blame a guy for trying." He pulled a card from his pocket. "If you see or hear anything, give me a call. We may be a backwater, but people here care about their neighbors."

"Did you know the victim?" I asked. Two could play at casual interrogation.

"Eloise Blackwell?" Okay, he had her name. "No. Not personally. From what I hear, she kept herself to herself. Hadn't been here long." He kept walking. "Ask Mavis. She tried to interview her when she first took the job. Woman refused to be interviewed. Odd, don't you think?"

Yep. I did think it odd. "Some people don't like the limelight."

"Not you, though, luckily. When you've got your breath

back, I'd like to do a profile on you. You're the closest we've got to a local competitor."

"Sure," I agreed. He was doing me a favor. The least I could do was chat to him about my experience on the show.

MAVIS CRANE HAD an office in what would once have been a bedroom. Trim said he was down the hall and after introducing us, left us alone. I let out a sigh. If they'd worked in close quarters, I'd have had to be more careful in my questions, as he clearly had a sharp brain along with a good memory.

Mavis seemed less daunting. She had to be long past normal retirement age. Pleasantly plump with deep-set brown eyes and short gray hair, she was wearing green overalls and a thin red cotton scarf tied in a nonchalant fashion around her neck. She greeted me with a wide smile. "Hello, dear," she said loudly. "Welcome."

She sat behind an old wooden schoolteacher's desk with paper all over it in neat piles. A computer sat on a side table, and there were photos, lists of all sorts, a huge calendar with scribbles all over it, and stacks of newspapers.

I smelled dust, newsprint and old building. "How can I help you?"

As she beckoned me closer, I immediately got the sense that not many people wandered through her doors. She appeared to be so pleased to see me, I suddenly felt bad for turning up empty-handed like a rude dinner guest.

"I'm looking for information on someone local." Her face was crinkled with lines. I had a vision suddenly of a large family, aunts and uncles talking over one another, rowdy siblings, children crawling over her. I was sure there was a loving spouse at home—she exerted the kind of confidence someone only had when they felt truly loved. "I'm here to uncover some local history."

"Writer, are you? Researching a novel? A little historical drama perhaps? Goodness knows we've had enough of that round here to fill a trilogy."

I chuckled. "Not a writer, no. I'm looking for ..." I stopped. How much information did I really want to give away to a stranger? I decided to go with the line I'd first given Katie Donegal when I began poking my nose into the staffing history of Broomewode Hall. "I'm looking for information about a distant cousin who might have lived in the area about twenty-five years ago." I paused. "A young man."

"A cousin, you say?"

"Of my mother's. I don't even have a name."

Mavis's mouth pursed. "You do know we're not MI5, right? Or a private detective service."

I nodded, even though her sarcasm wasn't exactly what I needed right now. "Yup. I'm looking for someone deceased."

Immediately her expression switched to one of compassion. "I'm sorry, luvvie. I didn't mean to make light of your search. I've lived here all my life. I might remember him."

"It would save me searching the obituaries for a youngish man who might have passed away in those years."

"That's a lot of ground you need to cover," Mavis said, "but maybe I can help you narrow things down a bit before you start looking through the papers? It's fair to say I know a lot about Broomewode Village history."

The clock was ticking, and I'd promised my baking pals

that I'd join them at the inn for our usual Sunday evening sendoff. So I cleared my throat and launched right into it, trying to describe my birth dad's ghost as though I'd seen him in a photo.

"I don't know his name, but I saw a photograph once. The man I'm looking for was tall and slender. Young, maybe in his mid-twenties or early thirties, with light brown hair swept back. He had smooth, tanned skin and a nice smile. A little bit cheeky-looking."

"He sounds nice, pet. Now lemme have a think."

Would Mavis be able to supply the information I'd been dreaming about? I opened the note function on my phone ready to take some notes.

"Hmm, it could be Fred, Alice's youngest, who died in a motor accident. That was in 2003. October. I remember because it was the month after my niece had her gallbladder surgery," Mavis suggested. "I think he was more like nineteen, though. Definitely on the younger side. I'd have said they knew all their cousins, but these days, with all that internet ancestry, it's amazing the surprises people get." She glanced at me hurriedly. "I'm sure this would be a pleasant one. Lovely people, Alice and her family."

I couldn't imagine the ghost who appeared to me in magic circles being only nineteen, but I figured it might be hard to tell when his edges were flickering and he was hovering above the ground like a hologram.

"You wouldn't think you'd forget young men who died before their time. Well, there was Joe. Betsy's boy that had the funny eye. Joined the army. Killed in Afghanistan, he was. Poor Betsy. It nearly killed her."

"I don't think he was in the army," I said quietly, almost

scared to interrupt her reminiscences. "I think he'd have died between 1994 and maybe 2000."

"The poor young viscount died in 1995, but I doubt he'd be your cousin. His family is famous and well-documented. Terrible thing, poor lad. With all he had to live for. A riding accident it was. He's buried in the local churchyard. A lovely monument."

I knew this story. I didn't have a lot of time to reminisce about local history. I wasn't looking for British aristocrats, more like the kind of bloke you'd find down the local pub enjoying a nice pint of traditional ale.

"Of course, there was the Doncasters' son Brian. Very sad that was. He was training to be a doctor. Not quite thirty. Brain aneurism."

Oh, that sounded promising. To think if my dad had lived, he might have been a doctor, which sounded so respectable. Then Mavis shook her head. "But that was in 1993. Too early."

I didn't want to give up Dr. Dad so easily. "Are you certain Brian died in 1993?"

"Oh, yes. It was the Queen's fortieth year on the throne. We were organizing a village party. Brian died that very day. You don't forget a thing like that."

"We think he was dating a girl named Valerie who worked in the kitchen of Broomewode."

Her eyes grew sharper. "Valerie. She was friendly with my daughter Joanna. They were the same age, you see. Used to meet up at the pub. Go to concerts together. I'm sure she was one of a group of them that went to Glastonbury together. To the music festival."

My heart began to pound. I'd come looking for my father,

but perhaps I was getting closer to finding my mother. "How old is Joanna?"

"She'll be forty-seven in August." She shook her head. "Hard to believe how quickly time passes. My girl, forty-seven, with grown children of her own."

Unknowingly, Mavis had given me my mother's age. And a lead on someone who'd known her well. "Is Joanna still in Broomewode?"

"No. They moved to Bristol, but you could telephone her. I'm sure she'd be glad to talk of the old days. And she might remember better who Valerie was dating."

"Is she still in touch with Valerie?" I felt like the very air in this overcrowded fire hazard of a room was holding its breath, but she shook her head, looking sorrowful. "No. Valerie left without a word. Joanna was awfully upset. She kept expecting to hear, but she never did. Of course, everybody wasn't on Instagram and Snapchat and I don't know what else, not in those days. They barely had email."

She wrote down her daughter's phone number and email address for me and gave me her business card. "I'll have a think about young men who passed away, shall I?"

"Yes, please." I gave her my contact details.

"You might want to look through the archives after all. My memory's not what it was."

I thought it was brilliant, and I told her so.

She leaned forward and laid her hand over mine. "I hope you find him, dear."

How obvious must I appear? She was too delicate to press me, but she knew I was looking for my father. I hadn't fooled her for a second.

"I hope so, too." I allowed myself to imagine what it would

have been like to meet my dad for the first time. It was easy to conjure up the nervous energy I knew such a meeting would bring. Maybe we would have arranged to meet at a restaurant or a café. Somewhere neutral where we could both feel relaxed. Maybe I'd hang back before entering—watch him sitting at the table, waiting for me. Would he dress up for the occasion? Put on a smart pair of trousers and a freshly pressed shirt? Or be more laid-back in his attire? Jeans and a T-shirt, perhaps? It was hard to imagine the image of my dad without thinking of the ghost and that strange brown robe he wore. At least I'd heard his speaking voice. Gentle but firm, a touch of lightheartedness to its tone. Would I be so nervous that I could barely speak, my tongue tied, a torrent of emotions flooding through me as I tried to introduce myself? Would I be scared of saying something too stupid? Or would my mouth run away with itself, burning with a thousand questions: what he did for a living, where he grew up, how he met my mother. Did he love her? Did he know about me?

A meeting like that would change my life forever.

"Maybe he didn't die," she said softly.

I nodded, feeling stunned and like I'd lost something I didn't even know that I'd had.

$\mathcal{I}$t was surreal being back at the inn with everyone crowded round me. I'd spent the last hour lost in the past, and now I had to act like my biggest woe was being voted off *The Great British Baking Contest*. The pub was busy and noisy—so different from the newspaper office. I tried to shake off the feeling that I'd brought the past in here with me, wearing history like a heavy cloak.

It was also strange being on the other side of the goodbye drinks. I was accustomed to commiserating with the losing contestant, wrapping them in hugs, offering consoling words. And now it was my turn. It felt like a strange dream that I'd wake up from any moment.

"We really love you, Poppy," Florence was saying.

"It's not going to be the same," Hamish added. "I'm still amazed it wasn't me sent home. It had to be close as a whisker."

"I will miss you," Gaurav said quietly.

"It's been a real pleasure," Maggie added. "But you're so

young yet. We haven't heard the last of you, Poppy Wilkinson, of that I'm sure."

I was so touched, on the cusp of becoming a blubbering mess. I truly felt cherished. So I thanked them all and said it was time to get the fizz in. We needed to celebrate Maggie's Star Baker status and toast my journey on *The Great British Baking Contest*.

At the bar, Eve greeted me with tears in her eyes. "You're not coming back next weekend, are you?"

I shook my head and took her hands, feeling that familiar charge of energy that reminded me we were bound together as coven sisters. "But I'm going to visit all the time. You won't be able to stop me." I lowered my voice. "Now that I know I'm part of a coven, I could never turn my back on my sisters. You're family. And family means everything to me. Everything."

Eve smiled sadly and wiped the tears from her eyes. "I really thought with Eloise's help you'd be fine." She glanced towards the kitchen. The police tape was gone, but I suspected the crime scene hadn't finished. "I guess nothing went well this weekend."

"I think I have a clue about Eloise's identity," I whispered.

Eve handed me an ice bucket and a bottle of prosecco. "Really? The whole terrible affair has been playing on my mind. I feel so guilty about not knowing anything about poor Eloise. I should have made more of an effort."

I nodded and said I felt the same but now I might have a lead. I told Eve about the best turf cakes in York comment.

"That's your lead?" Eve didn't sound as though Scotland Yard could close its doors now that I was on the scene.

Maybe she was right and I was looking for clues where

there weren't any. "I'll mention it anyway, maybe, in case it's useful."

"Of course, love. You do that."

I walked back to the table and set down the bucket. Gaurav collected champagne flutes, and I popped the bottle. The sound was usually one I associated with celebrations, not commiserations, and then when I started to think about sad things, Eloise's unsolved death began to plague me. Maybe the turf cake thing meant nothing, but I quickly whipped out my phone and sent Sgt. Lane a message.

Think I have a lead about where Eloise might have lived before she came to the village. Has anyone mentioned York? She may have worked there before Broomewode Inn.

I put my phone away before anyone told me off for being distracted and poured the fizz. Hamish handed round the bubbling flutes. "You okay, Poppy?" he asked quietly. "Not too disappointed, I hope?"

"No. It's not that." I told him I thought I had a lead about Eloise. But before I could share my hunch, Florence led the clinking of glasses.

"Here's to Poppy! We'll miss you!"

When everyone had settled down, I decided to put my questions about turf cakes to the team. Five bakers were better than one.

But before I could speak, Florence suddenly stood up and waved manically at the entrance of the pub. Talk about breaking a girl's stride. I turned to see what had taken the attention away from my investigation yet again. It was Stanley, the producer from London, and Florence's new squeeze.

He smiled, waved, and then confidently strode towards our table. Florence introduced him to our group. She was so flushed, she was positively giddy with pride.

I caught Hamish's eye. He looked amused. But I wasn't in the mood for play. I needed to ask the bakers a serious question, so as soon as the pleasantries were over, I steered the conversation to turf cakes.

"Ooh, now those take me back," said Maggie.

"You know what they are?"

"Oh yes. My Nan was from Whitby, north Yorkshire—they're famous round those parts. They're a kind of rock cake. Absolutely delicious."

"I know those!" Hamish said excitedly. "Simple but tasty. They're buttery flat cakes. Spiced with nutmeg, cinnamon, and citrus peels. Kind of like an all-year-round Christmas flavor. They say the best ones are in York."

My heart began to beat wildly. Was I onto something here with the turf cakes beyond a delicious dessert? Had Eloise worked somewhere in Yorkshire, where she was famous for making turf cakes? Surely this would narrow down the police's search. I was about to ask more when Darius interrupted us, asking if the gentleman would like a drink. His voice was clipped, not his usual smooth, relaxed manner. I saw him flick a glance from Stanley's possessive arm to Florence's face. She pretended not to notice.

It was difficult to act naturally and not let on there was something between him and Florence. Not that Florence was batting a thickly painted eyelash. She didn't seem uncomfortable in the least.

I turned towards Darius. Even though he was smiling, he looked furious. A shiver went down my spine. I was surprised

Florence had invited the producer to join us at the inn knowing it was likely Darius would be working. Clearly Darius was invested in Florence. It must hurt like hell to see her fawning over another man. How could she not be embarrassed with both men in the room like this? I never would have been able to keep my cool. Not that I would ever manage to juggle two men. Or ever had the chance, come to think of it. Or the desire to.

Benedict walked in at that moment, glanced around and, when he spotted me, headed my way. My phone signaled an incoming text. From Sgt. Lane. "Nice work, partner." It was just jokey enough that a person might consider the words flirtatious if they had a mind to.

I put the phone down as Benedict approached. With a nod for the rest of the group, he focused on me. "I heard what happened. Bad luck."

"Thanks. But, in a way it's a relief." Nearly every person who'd left the show had said these words. I'd assumed they were only showing a brave face, but I really did feel relief at letting go of the stress of the show, of constantly striving to create something spectacular under pressure.

"We'll miss you. I was wondering if—"

"Ben, don't hog Poppy," Florence said, pushing a glass of bubbly at him. "We're having a last drink with our friend before we lose her forever. Oh, and you must meet Stanley."

Benedict accepted the drink and reached out to shake Stanley's hand. If Florence had been nearer, I'd have kicked her ankle under the table. I would really have liked to know how that question would have ended. "Poppy, I was wondering if ..." So many possibilities.

Now I was wondering, too.

"And bring another glass for Stanley," she said to Darius. Ouch. How could she order him around like that? She must know he was hurting. Talk about adding insult to injury.

Darius said he'd be right back. He was polite, but it was so obviously forced that the mood of the table tangibly shifted.

When Darius left, Florence laughed her pretty laugh and told Stanley that Benedict would one day inherit all of Broomewode.

"Take it from me. Lot of work. I've an estate in the north. Money pit, that's what it is."

Benedict agreed, and Stanley immediately launched into a story about dry rot. Florence moved closer to me and whispered in my ear, "Darius is being a real drag. He's been texting me alllll day. I thought he understood this was only a bit of fun. But he's gone all jealous and clingy. Not what I signed on for."

I raised an eyebrow. *Obviously* Darius was jealous, but I didn't have time to dwell on Florence's love life. I only offered a shrug as consolation and then turned to Maggie and asked if she'd tell me more about turf cakes.

"Why? Have you heard something? Will we need to make them?"

"No. I was just wondering where I'd go if I wanted to taste the best ones." I shrugged. "I've suddenly got a lot more free time."

She patted my hand, and once more I felt like one of her grandchildren after they'd taken a tumble. "My favorite part is the lovely cherries and almonds on top," Maggie said. "And for the best turf cakes in York, you go to Lester's Cake Shop."

The best turf cakes in York.

The exact words Eloise had used. It was a long shot, but I wondered if they might know her at the bakery.

"Oh no," Florence said.

I turned to face her. "What is it?"

"You've got that look on your face again. That 'Poppy's about to go off and do something dangerous' look."

I burst out laughing. "Nothing dangerous. I need to make a quick phone call. But I promise to come right back and continue the celebrations."

"You've been here all of ten minutes, Poppy Wilkinson," Florence chided.

Hamish shot me a worried glance. "Need help?"

"Not yet, but I might."

Benedict turned to look at me, but Stanley was enthusiastically describing the renovations he was making, and Benedict was obviously too polite to stop him.

I excused myself again and went up to my bedroom, where I could make a call in private. Thankfully, Gerry wasn't waiting for me when I turned the key, as was his usual wont. I breathed a sigh of relief. He could be helpful, but right now I needed to focus and get my best charm on.

I took a seat on Gateau's favorite armchair and searched online for Lester's Cake Shop in York. With a couple of taps, I found an old-fashioned-looking website and breathed a sigh of relief when I found a contact number at the bottom of their homepage. I carefully tapped in the digits.

As the phone rang, Gateau scampered in through the open window and came to sit on my lap. As much as I loved seeing my friendly familiar, her sudden appearance made me cautious. She liked a good snuggle, that was for sure. But she came to me when I was sad or in danger. Maybe something about this call might have triggered her instincts. I decided to use an alias, just in case.

"Hello, Lester's Cake Shop. Lester speaking. How can I help?"

The voice belonged to a jolly-sounding man, maybe in his sixties. A granddad perhaps. But if I'd learned anything these last few weeks, it was that people could be seriously deceptive.

"Oh hello," I said, affecting a fake British accent and employing the alias I'd used when first trying to get into Broomewode Hall in my first week at the Village. "My name is Tabitha Worth. I'm a food writer." I mentioned a top magazine. "I'm working on a feature about the bakers behind the scenes who make the most iconic treats in the UK. Could I speak to the baker who makes your famous turf cakes?"

The man cleared his throat. "That's great to hear. The baker's new, I'm afraid. He's only been here a couple of months, so if you're looking for more background—"

"Oh, yes. I was told it was a woman who'd made your cakes famous. I can't quite read my scribbled notes. Was her name Eloise?"

"Ella." He chuckled. "You might want to work on that handwriting. "Ella Cartwright. Wonderful baker, but as I say, doesn't work here anymore."

"I'm really sorry to hear that." And I was. It seemed my crazy hunch had been correct, and now I knew more about the woman I'd known as Eloise.

I wanted to pry but had no idea what to ask next. I thought of "Trim" Trimble asking the awkward question anyway, hoping I'd tell him what he wanted to know. I'd have to act like a real reporter too.

But I didn't have to. Before I could say another word, Lester said, "And please don't think she left because of anything I said or did. I was gutted to lose her."

"Why did she leave?" He could hang up, he could tell me to mind my own business, or he could answer me.

"You've obviously been around enough bakers, Tabitha— okay if I call you Tabitha?"

"Yes."

"Well, like I say, when you've been around bakers, you get to know they can be an insecure lot."

"I've definitely experienced that," I agreed, thinking of the last six weeks.

"Ella was a good baker, kept herself to herself, but she had a difficult home life."

"I'm sorry to hear that."

"The best turf cake baker I've ever had the pleasure to work with. Not such a sure hand when it came to men." He sighed. "I told her not to marry him. It was too quick, I said, but they don't listen."

"She was married?" I blurted out.

"Still is, far as I know. He swept her off her feet, wouldn't take no for an answer until she married him. So happy she was, I was glad she hadn't listened to me, and then suddenly, POOF, things changed. He left her. Simply said he was done. I didn't want to be right, but I was right all along. Poor Ella was beside herself. She was determined to get him back, so she left her job to follow him. Should have said good riddance if you ask me."

"Any idea where she went?" Was it possible I'd got it wrong?

"Down south somewhere. That's all I know. Told her she

could have her job back if it didn't work out. I keep expecting she'll call."

I didn't want to be the one to tell him that probably wasn't going to happen.

I couldn't believe that Eloise—Ella—was married. No wonder she was moody at work: She was heartbroken. The poor girl.

But if they were the same person, and she came south to find her husband, where was he?

CHAPTER 15

*A*fter I'd finished the call, I stared out of the window of my bedroom at the inn for what was probably the last time. Evening was settling in, with gorgeous splashes of pink and orange across the skies.

I couldn't get over how Eloise, or Ella, had hidden so much pain from her co-workers. Her heart had been broken. She'd been desperate to find the husband who'd swept her off her feet and then disappeared. She'd packed up everything in York, left her job, put her life on hold. And her search had led to Broomewode Village. Which surely meant that her husband must live nearby? Why else take a job at the local inn?

I tried to bring to mind everyone I'd met who lived here, what their stories were, whether they'd been born here or had moved more recently. I ticked off each person one by one. It was a mixed list. On the one hand, Broomewode Village had a longstanding community of families who'd been here generations: the Champneys and all the generations before them, dear Eileen and dastardly Penelope, Katie Donegal, the old gamekeeper Mitty and his somewhat questionable family. But on the other hand, the village attracted new blood, those looking to escape the city. Eve and Susan immediately came to mind—but the vortex had likely brought them here to be with their sisters. Susan Bentley and her husband had also moved to Broomewode in retirement, as had her new friend Reginald—but surely he was far too old for Eloise? Who else could be a contender for Eloise's affections?

And then I remembered Hamish's devasting tip from the police. Edward. I'd obviously pushed his name out of my mind, not wanting to believe that he could be capable of something so terrible. Edward was also a newbie in Broomewode, or at least at his job—joining the gardening team soon after I arrived in Broomewode. He was the right age for Eloise, mid- to late twenties, and he'd said he'd left home to find work. Was it possible he moved to get away from a wife? I thought he'd told me he was from Devon, but it was an easy lie, to swap York for Devon, and he didn't have a distinguishable accent, just slightly Somerset, and that could have lingered from childhood. If he'd moved around from town to town, whatever his real accent was could have easily diluted.

He'd certainly seemed very upset at the news of her death. Could it be fear masquerading as sadness? Fear that he'd be caught?

He'd been spending time with Lauren from the ill-fated wedding, after all. What if he was one of those serial monogamists, moving from one intense relationship to another? Or a love addict? Addicted to the first thrills of falling in love, which never lasted. Perhaps he'd been careless in the pursuit of the ultimate adrenaline rush, the burst of oxytocin. He had admitted to bumping into Eloise last night, but it wasn't until Sol the chef spoke to the police that it came to light that he'd taken the meat for Edward to cook dinner for Eloise. Why had he lied about their interaction and tried to downplay it? It made him look so guilty. If he was the last person to see Eloise before she died, then of course he'd be a prime suspect. Especially if I now revealed that he was her estranged husband, furious that she'd followed him across the country.

My palms were clammy, and my heart beat furiously. I was still trying to resist the notion that Edward was a bad guy. I liked him a lot. He was friendly and kind. Or so I thought.

Surely by now I knew not to be ruled by emotion when it came to narrowing down suspects? It was always the people you least suspected would let you down that eventually did. That's what made it burn so bad.

I had to know if Edward had been Eloise's husband. I had to know if he had it in him to kill.

There was only way to find out without confronting him and putting myself in serious danger. With trembling hands, I redialed the number to Lester's Bakery.

The phone rang for what seemed an inordinate amount of time. With each new ring, my heart moved another inch towards my throat. I both did and didn't want an answer. I was about to hang up when the phone clicked.

"Hello, Lester's Bakery."

I swallowed. It was time to face the music—for real this time.

I let my British alias go and explained to poor Lester that I was, in fact, an American by the name of Poppy who'd met Eloise in the local inn and spoke with her at length about bread.

Lester was baffled—as well he might be.

"Okay, dear. I'm not quite sure that I'm following," he said slowly.

I took a breath. "I was worried about revealing too much just now. You can never be too careful. It's just that ..." I took another breath. "Eloise, I mean Ella, well, she's dead."

Lester gasped. "Is this a joke? Some kind of sick, awful prank?"

"No. I would never joke about something this serious. She died yesterday in the kitchen at the pub under pretty suspicious circumstances. It looked like an accident, but I'm not so sure, and neither are the police. Not a single person knew she was married. And I'm worried that she caught up with her husband and he didn't like it ... maybe enough to do something about it ... permanently."

"I can't believe it," Lester said quickly. "Such a sweet girl. So happy. So in love. And an absolute blinder of a baker. What a loss."

Sol and Darius's comments about Eloise couldn't have been further from Lester's warm summation. They'd called her moody and difficult; Eve had said she'd kept herself to herself. If this was what being in love looked like, then I wanted nothing to do with it.

"It is a great loss," I echoed. "Which is why we need to get to the bottom of this whole tragic affair. If foul play was at work, then we have to find the culprit."

Lester was silent for a moment, obviously still in shock. I stared out of my window, watching the sun make its path across the deepening sky.

"What can I do?" he said, finally clearing his throat. "I'll help in any way I can."

"Who was her husband?"

"Wait, you don't think—"

"It's possible he really didn't want her to find him."

"I'd like to personally turf his cake," Lester said.

I smiled. My instinct hadn't been wrong about Lester. He was a good egg. If only I could say the same about Edward.

"I wish I could help you, but I never met the fellow. Another thing that made me suspicious. Saw some photos of their honeymoon. Good-looking chap."

Right now I needed to make sure Ella and Eloise were indeed one and the same. "I was hoping you might have a photo of Ella? I need to make sure I've got this right and the woman I met as Eloise is definitely Ella."

Lester agreed immediately and said he was sure he had one on his phone.

"If only I had one of her husband. If only I'd known." He put me on speaker as he scoured his phone for photographs. In the background, I could hear the hubbub of the bakery, faint sounds of customers talking and the crinkling of brown paper bags.

"How could you?" I said, trying to make Lester realize that all of this stuff was so out of our hands. There was no sense in going through the what-ifs; it would only make you crazy. For my part, I was feeling increasingly guilty about falling asleep when I should have been downstairs meeting up with Eloise. If I had been the reason she was in the pantry all alone, it didn't bear thinking about.

"I don't suppose you know anything about Ella's family?" I asked hopefully.

"No." He sighed. "She didn't really talk about her family. Said she'd moved around a lot. She seemed kind of lonely before she met this bloke. I suppose it made her a prime target to be taken advantage of. A lonely girl in a big city."

I suddenly felt very emotional. Lester was right; you *were* more vulnerable without your family around you. I missed my parents terribly. And I was already missing my baking family from the show and my coven sisters from the village. The idea of not seeing them every single weekend was beginning to sink in.

But now was not the time to let my emotions get the better of me. I had to focus on uncovering the mystery of Ella's death. Lester said he had to hang up to message me the photograph, so I gave him my number, and he promised to hit send as soon we hung up.

I put the phone down for a moment and stroked Gateau, who'd fallen fast asleep on more than her fair share of the chair. She rolled onto her back and offered me her belly for tickles. She mewed a little and stretched as I stroked her soft black fur.

Lester didn't disappoint. A few moments later, my phone dinged. I snatched it from the bed and eagerly unlocked the screen. There was a message from an unknown number. "Is this her?" the message read.

I scrolled down, and there was a photograph of a young woman in a floury apron, holding a tray of what I assumed must be turf cakes, brown hair in a messy bun and a proud smile on her face. I breathed out. Both triumphant and very sad.

The woman smiling at me was Eloise.

I replied immediately, confirming that it was the women I'd met. Lester replied a second later. *Part of me was hoping you'd got the wrong lass.*

Me too, Lester. Me too.

Now I had to get my hands on a photograph of Edward. If I could send it to Lester and have him confirm that he was Ella's husband, then I'd be one step closer to finding out what really happened to Ella in the pantry, even if that meant discovering something terrible about my friend. Until then, I could hope that it wasn't Edward.

It could have been any of the eligible men in Broome-wode. Could the animosity between Eloise and the chef have actually been a marital spat? But no. Sol had mentioned a wife. Unless it was a bigamous wife. Now that would be inconvenient.

But why would he hire his ex and then kill her? It made no sense.

How about Darius? Although he and Florence were attached at the hip—it would be strange if Eloise's husband was *that* blatant about being with another woman. I'd try to snap a furtive photo of them all and ping them back to Lester. The sooner I eliminated suspects, the better. I sent Lester a quick message to tell him my plan.

He texted back warning me that he'd only glimpsed the fellow in a photo. He wasn't sure he'd recognize him.

Well, we had to try.

Phone still in hand, I raced downstairs to tell Hamish what I'd found out and begin my little photography project.

THE PUB WAS BUSIER than when I left it. There was no food service, obviously, but it was still full. I suspected people had come to gossip about the murder and maybe have a ghoulish look at the place where Eloise had been killed. I couldn't help but feel another pang of regret at having to leave this place.

There was a long queue at the bar. People round here must be thirsty for a cold pint of cider. But when I looked closely, I saw that poor Eve was on her own. There was no sign of Darius. Hmm. My first photo was going to be hard to snap.

I went over. "You okay?" I mouthed.

She nodded grimly. "Darius went out for a cigarette break ages ago. Lazy so-and-so."

I offered to help, but Eve declined. "Bunch of ghouls," she said. "A little waiting never hurt anyone."

Then Sol came around the bar and called, "Who's next?"

Eve looked at him in surprise. I didn't suppose he did much bartending, but he couldn't cook in his kitchen, so at least he was helping.

Was he gallant for not reporting Eloise's money troubles and invoice skimming to the inn's owners, or had he been holding it over her, waiting for a chance of blackmail? Or what if he was actually her husband, pretending not to know her? A shiver went through me. How could someone be so callous? She'd told him she'd recently lost a great deal of money. Who had better access to her funds than her husband?

I pulled out my phone and, angling it from my hip, snapped a sneaky pic before he turned his back to reach for a glass.

I looked down at the image. Sol was partially obscured by people in the queue for the bar, but it was a decent enough side image—enough for Lester to be able to tell if this was Eloise's husband.

I quickly sent the photo to Lester along with the line, "Was this him?"

I put my phone away and prayed for a quick response. A simple yes or no would help narrow my search. I returned to the bakers, who appeared to be enthralled by a story Stanley was telling.

I resumed my place and nudged Hamish.

"What is it?" he whispered.

In a low voice, I told him everything I'd learned from Lester—Eloise's real name, that she'd worked in York, and that she'd left in pursuit of a husband who'd abandoned her. As I spoke, Hamish's eyes widened. "You found out all that in the last twenty minutes?"

I nodded. "Lucky guess."

"I'd like to take you up to Scotland with me and give you a job."

"Thanks, but I'm strictly amateur. I knew her and want to see her killer brought to justice."

"Poor girl," he murmured. "She'd been through a lot."

I nodded and finished by saying that we needed to tell the police.

"Agreed," Hamish replied, his mouth set in a firm line.

Stanley's story came to an end, and the others looked at Hamish and I like we were two old fishwives rudely gibbering on in the corner. It was then that I noticed that Stanley's biggest fan was missing. "Where's Florence?" I asked, pointing at the seat where her cashmere cardigan was casually draped across the arm.

"She left ages ago, come to think of it," Hamish replied.

"Just said she was popping to the ladies' room," Stanley said.

"She's probably still powdering her nose," Maggie said, tapping her own nose lightly. "She's a lady who likes to look after herself. But tell us, did you find what you were looking for at Lester's Bakery?"

I nodded grimly, unsure of how much to divulge to the group before speaking to the police. My phone pinged. I whipped it out. Bingo. It was Lester. But when I clicked open his text, my heart sank. I hadn't nailed the suspect first time round. "Nope," the message said. "Bloke was younger."

"Ooh, I'd love a turf cake right now," Maggie continued, a nostalgic look on her face. "Lester's really is the best bakery in those parts."

"Is it near Yorvik Viking Center?" Gaurav asked. "I think I was there once. It's not too far from Birmingham."

Yorvik Viking Center? Why did that sound so familiar?

And then I remembered. It was the logo on Darius's T-shirt yesterday.

Darius. The handsome Greek flirt who hadn't worked in Broomewode much longer than Eloise.

Darius. Who had just disappeared from the bar, leaving Eve in the lurch.

Darius. Who was fuming about Florence's new gentleman friend.

I was getting a very bad feeling behind my breastbone.

"How long did you say Florence has been gone?" I asked abruptly.

Everyone immediately stopped talking about York. Gaurav checked his watch. "At least fifteen minutes ago."

Far too long to just refresh a swipe of lipstick or fluff up her curls.

"Actually, I don't think Florence is in the loo," Gaurav

suddenly piped up. "I went myself just a few minutes ago and I saw her talking with—" He stopped and glanced at Stanley, then looked as though he wished he'd kept his mouth shut. "With someone in the corridor."

"Was it Darius?" I asked.

Gaurav looked at me like I was being inappropriate. "I think so. Not that I'm well acquainted with our waiter."

"Oh no!" I cried, leaping up from the table, upsetting Hamish's glass so that the remainder of his drink spooled across the oak, turning it a darker shade of brown. Darius was dangerous. I had to find Florence before it was too late.

CHAPTER 16

*A*ll of a sudden, the pub felt too noisy, too busy, too full of locals. Guffaws and shrieks shot through me like shards of glass. The room went cold and still as if visited by a haunted soul. Could I feel Eloise's angry spirit? Was she here, reproachful about us taking too long to figure out her story? Surely not, if Gerry had indeed seen her pass over. My mind spun, tripping over itself with wild thoughts I couldn't contain. *Please don't let it be Florence I'm feeling. Don't let her be gone. Please, no.*

"Poppy?" Benedict asked worriedly. "What is it? You're as white as a ghost!"

The other bakers, Benedict and Stanley all stood up from the table alongside me. I'd clean forgotten that I was surrounded by people and stared back at him. "It's Darius," I said. "I think he's dangerous. As in deadly dangerous. We need to find Florence *immediately*. Gaurav, did you see if Florence and Darius were leaving the pub?"

Gaurav shook his head. "I only noticed the two of them because their conversation looked intense. I figured"—

Gaurav lowered his voice, but it was no use; Stanley could hear everything—"it was a lovers' tiff."

Trust Gaurav to pick up on the signs and stay discreet. I couldn't even keep my mouth shut in front of Florence. *Florence*. I snapped back to attention. "We need to figure out where they might have gone."

I looked at Maggie, Gaurav, Hamish and Stanley, hoping they might have a clue where Florence might go to have a quarrel or difficult conversation with a lover. But they stared back with blank faces. Stanley just looked shocked, as well he might. Did he have any idea that Florence was such a femme fatale? He was probably wondering what on earth he'd gotten into, agreeing to drive all the way here from London. Suddenly, Hamish suggested they might have gone for a walk in the grounds. "If Darius had bad intentions, he'd suggest going outside. Try to get her as far away from other people as possible."

The group looked glum. "But that's such a huge area," Maggie said. "We'll never be able to cover it all."

"We have to try," I urged. "She can't have gone too far. Florence isn't one for hurrying," I added, trying to dispel the feeling of dread, which was growing deeper and more disturbing as each minute passed. But I couldn't bring myself to give a hopeful smile. It was like each cell in my body, one after another, was slowly catching on to my fear, and each time the fear spread it mutated, becoming stronger and more potent.

"I've got the key to her room," Stanley piped up. "She gave it to me earlier so I could drop off my overnight bag. I'll search her things, see if there's anywhere in the village that she likes to visit—a place she might suggest to Darius to calm him down. It's a long shot, but it might narrow the search. I'll catch you up."

Hamish said that was an excellent idea. I was really surprised Stanley was taking all this so well. He was calm and pragmatic. I felt bad for wondering if he might have been married before. It wasn't nice to jump to conclusions about people just from their demeanor.

Without thinking, I grabbed Florence's cashmere cardigan and held it close. My nose filled with the scent of her powdery perfume. I closed my eyes. *Where are you, Florence?*

"I know the grounds as well as anyone, I suppose," Benedict said. "I'll go with you."

We left the pub, Florence's cardigan still in my hands. Outside, the weather was still warm, the sun casting the last of her rays down on our frantic search party. Maggie called out Florence's name, and we all followed suit, circling the inn's perimeter, hoping that she hadn't ventured too far.

"Florence?" Hamish called in his deep baritone voice. "Where are you?"

Gaurav echoed his call until we were all saying her name, the air filling with the sound of our collective worry. Surely she could hear us? Had they really gotten that far away from the pub? I cursed myself for speaking to Lester for so long. I'd lost precious minutes upstairs while Florence was being cornered by Darius.

We stopped walking for a moment and fell quiet, hoping to hear a response, however distant or quiet it might be. The blood rushed in my ears. Nothing. The silence was louder than our calls.

"Should we split up?" Gaurav suggested.

I knew that it would make looking easier, but as worried as I was about Florence's safety, I didn't want to put anyone else in danger either. If I was right about Darius, then sending someone else straight into his orbit was a big mistake. Huge.

"We'll find her," Benedict said, sounding calm and confident. I never thought I'd be so glad to have him around, apart from when he saved my life, that is.

"You're right," I said, pulling myself together. "No one knows the land here better than you. Where might two people be hiding if they didn't want to be found?"

Benedict scratched his forehead. "There are a hundred places like that around here."

The dread in my body was still growing, and I was beginning to feel crushed under its weight. Darius was an obsessive. Lester had told me he wooed Ella until she agreed to marry him, much quicker than Lester felt comfortable with. If Darius was obsessed with Florence and had seen that she'd moved on within twenty-hours of sharing his bed, then what might he do? Darius had clearly thought nothing of marrying Eloise and then disappearing to a new part of the country and starting again. Could he have been so upset by Eloise trying to get in between him and his new romance that he'd cornered her in the kitchen on Friday? If Gerry was right and there were no loose bolts on the pantry floor, then someone had removed them on purpose. And if that someone was Darius, then Florence was with a murderer right now. Alone with a murderer. Not exactly the kind of situation you wanted your best baking friend to be in.

Benedict began listing good hiding places around the grounds, but I didn't have time for us to search them all. I knew that our best option was for me to try and somehow tune in to my powers as a witch.

I told the other bakers to work in pairs and search each place carefully, using Benedict's suggestions and starting from the inn and working out. I was grateful to have a whole team of people so willing to help right now. I told them I'd stay and see if Stanley had unearthed any clues in Florence's room.

The bakers told me to be careful, and I could see that Benedict was concerned. "Don't worry," I mouthed, as he turned back to look at me one more time.

He nodded grimly and took charge of the others. Hamish pulled out his phone and was probably putting in a call to DI Hembly, and I was relieved that soon the police would be on the alert. Knowing Hamish, he'd relay more about what I'd learned speaking to Lester at the bakery. I watched as the group disappeared around the corner.

I walked to the side of the inn until I stood at the beginning of the path that led to the magic circle. I didn't have time to walk there, but at least I could be facing its special energy.

I was still clutching Florence's cardigan, and then the words of Eve's spell suddenly flew into my head. I touched the soft fabric and tried to concentrate on Florence, her scent, her laughter, her certain *je ne sais quoi.*

> *Goddesses of the sun, earth, stars and moon,*
> *Lead me to Florence and please do it soon.*
> *Her life is in danger, of that I am sure.*
> *Help me find her by your light good and pure.*
> *So I will, so mote it be.*

I concentrated my energy, just like I did when opening locked doors or lighting a candle's wick, but this time turned the energy towards the image of Florence, imagining it as a ball of light. An electric force coursed through my body, beginning in my belly and reaching out to my toes and fingertips. I buzzed with the vibrations. I closed my eyes, trying to manifest the moment I'd find Florence safe and well, trying to will it into being, to *feel* the relief of finding her unharmed.

I don't know what I'd been expecting, but when I opened my eyes, everything looked the same. Was there some clue that my spell had worked? Did I feel more inclined to turn in one direction than another? Maybe some kind of magic light to appear and point me in the direction of a secret spot? I suddenly felt foolish. I didn't feel a thing, just even more drained from concentrating so hard and using my energy. I clearly didn't have enough control over my powers to be of any help. I hung my head in shame.

What use was being a witch if you couldn't use magic to help a friend in danger?

CHAPTER 17

$\mathcal{B}$ut now wasn't the time to let my emotions get the best of me. I had to stay strong and keep looking for Florence. Maybe my magic would work in ways that were still mysterious to me. I couldn't lose hope.

I turned back towards the inn and saw Benedict heading my way. He seemed taller somehow and more confident. After our unfortunate first meeting, where I'd thought he was a ghostly poser, I'd slowly come to accept that he was very much flesh and blood and pretty hot.

"Anything?" I called out hopefully.

But Benedict just shook his head. "I've sent the others to the most likely places, but I don't like leaving you alone. It's not safe. Have you had any luck?"

"I don't think so," I said quietly, ashamed that I didn't have better news to deliver.

I realized then that Benedict hadn't questioned me when I asked for a moment alone. And he wasn't asking now what I'd done while he'd set up the search party. Benedict wasn't an uncurious man. Was it possible that he ...? No. Of course not. Why on earth would Benedict suspect that I had any magical powers? He probably just thought I was a bit of a strange girl and was being kind about my eccentricity. Well, I'd take that over being outed as a witch.

I felt that dreadful despair creeping up on me again when suddenly a familiar sound pierced the air. It was the hawk! Had he heard my spell? Was this the sign that I was looking for?

I cupped my hands against the setting sun, and there he was: the hawk. *My* hawk, I was sure of it, with his lovely plume, the scattering of white on his rich brown body, the cinnamon-red of his tail. His beak was curved and sharp, and as he swooped down past us, I saw that his eyes were sharper, more focused than I'd ever noticed before. He let out a shrill call and swooped down ever lower, his speckled feathers spread out to make a wide, majestic fan, head angled forward in concentration, focused on something I couldn't see. Was he trying to tell me something?

"Come on," I said to Benedict, still looking skyward. "Let's get going."

"Are you seriously suggesting ..." Benedict tailed off, seeming to think better of questioning my harebrained ideas.

Obviously, I couldn't address Benedict's query. What would I say? Yes, the hawk has shown up to show us the way to Florence. And I think I might have called on him for help using my special powers. In fact, I think the hawk is attached to my birth dad, who might also happen to be magical? Not going to happen.

I followed the hawk's flight, not letting him slip from view. The sun was setting in the distance, and the hawk made a beautiful silhouette against the darkening sky. Benedict stayed beside me in a silence that I was surprised to find was comfortable. I was grateful that he didn't question my methods. I didn't want to explain myself while attempting to locate Florence through intuition and magic, and keep the dread at bay. I felt more attuned to Florence now that the hawk was here.

We were covering ground fast with the inn behind us, Susan's farm off to the right and the great Broomewode Hall ahead on our left. The baking tent's white awning caught the fading light and glowed.

But then the hawk changed direction. He turned away from the manor house and back towards us, hovering and circling a part of the grounds I'd never explored before. "I don't understand," I said to Benedict. "What is he circling? I can't see anything."

"There's an old cistern just beyond that cluster of trees," Benedict said, picking up the pace.

"A cistern?" I asked, almost breaking into a run trying to keep up with Benedict's long stride.

"Like a stone well hidden in the grounds. It used to act as a water reservoir in the old days, holding the water until it was needed for the house. It just collects rainwater now."

A well. *Of course* a crazed jealous lover would lure his target to a dark place below ground where it was a struggle to get out. I shivered. Florence must be so frightened.

I ran to keep up until we reached what I figured was the cistern, half hidden by a cluster of beech trees.

"Down here," he said, pointing to a ladder at the mouth of the stone structure. He took the first step and then reached out for my hand. I took it and let him lead the way. His grip was firm, and I was comforted by the size of his hand, how safe my own smaller one felt tucked in his.

"Be careful," he whispered, letting go of my hand. "The rungs are slippery. Keep a sure footing."

The inside of the cistern was damp and dank, an almost metallic smell rising up from the ancient stone. I could hear voices. They grew louder the farther we descended into the dark.

"That's Darius!" Benedict whispered.

I nodded grimly although he couldn't see me. It was Darius all right. I just hoped that we weren't too late.

"Go back," Benedict whispered, his face close to mine so he barely breathed the words. "Get help."

"I'm not leaving you here alone," I whispered back. I had powers he didn't know about. I could protect him.

We might have kept arguing, but a light appeared below us, and there were Darius and Florence, illuminated by a torch that Darius was waving about manically.

Florence was alive! I exhaled loudly.

Benedict skipped the bottom rung and landed with a thud on the ground. I quickly followed.

But it was as if we weren't there at all. Florence looked at us, terrified, but Darius didn't turn to face us. He was too busy ranting, and his voice was soaring with indignation, growing louder and more caustic, his words laced with vitriol.

"I love you, Florence. How could you be with another man? I won't stand for it. I won't allow it! You are mine. Do you hear? Mine. We are entwined, one person—not two."

As he spoke, Florence backed away farther into the wall.

"I'm going to marry you, Florence Cinelli," he suddenly declared.

Florence's eyes opened even wider, the whites shining in the dark.

Suddenly it all made sense. I stepped forward. "That's why you had to kill Ella, isn't it? So you could marry Florence?"

Darius spun round and glared at me. His eyes flashed, and he was sweating, no doubt from exerting all that energy declaring his undying love. Except that it was a dying love—it was just that someone else had to die in order to make room for it. What a coward.

I couldn't tell if Darius was angry or shocked. It was like he'd suddenly been roused from a fever dream and brought back down to earth. He was panting, and his arms were still out in front of him, ready to gesticulate alongside the next passionate decree of love.

But my words appeared to be sinking in. His tanned face was losing color—fast.

"What are you talking about? Why are you here? I'm trying to talk to my woman."

"*Your* woman?" Florence spat. "I'm not your anything, you crazy man!"

Florence looked at us in despair. "He made me climb down here. I was so scared. I thought he was jealous and I could talk him out of it, but it's not that. I think he's mad." Florence suddenly stopped talking as Darius took another step closer to her. She pinned herself flat against the wall.

"I'm talking about your wife, Ella," I said, trying to get Darius's attention away from Florence. It worked. He turned back towards me. I breathed a sigh of relief but tried to stay firm, holding my ground. "Or Eloise, as she called herself when she took the job as pastry chef at Broomewode Inn. That is, until she suddenly died."

"Eloise?" Florence said, bewildered. "You were married to the pastry chef? No wonder she was so rude to me."

Darius pointed at me. "She doesn't know what she's talking about."

"I think she does," Benedict interrupted. "And I think you should listen very carefully."

"It's an old story," I said quietly. "Man meets woman, falls desperately in love at first sight, sweeps woman off her feet and BOOM! Marries her quicker than you can say 'I do.' Except once you actually had her, Ella lost her sparkle. She wasn't a fresh shiny conquest anymore. She was a real living breathing human being with needs and vulnerabilities. And you couldn't handle it, could you? It's the thrill of the chase, the promise of the new that you want, Darius. So you left. Just like that. Packed up your things and disappeared."

"You are the crazy one," Darius said, his fevered eyes turning to Florence, beseeching.

I shook my head. "I'm not crazy, but I think Ella was a little love crazy. She'd made her marriage vows faithfully. She was so love in with you that she left her job and her life in York and came to find you. But when she did, what happened? You ignored her? Acted like you'd never met? I can't even imagine how devastating that must have been for her."

"Oh, poor Ella," Darius said, mimicking my voice. "Poor sad Ella. Ha! I gave that woman an experience of love that she *never* would have had if it weren't for me. I gave her a Hollywood-style relationship. The stuff that romance novels are made of. I gave her the dream. She could never have expected it to last. The moment we were married, I knew I'd made a mistake. Ella was so ordinary. So unremarkable. Not like you, Florence," he said, turning back to my friend. "You sparkle. You shine. You're my soul mate."

"So you're not even going to deny it," Benedict said quietly, shaking his head.

"Is it a crime to marry someone and then leave?" Darius retorted.

"No," I said firmly. "But it *is* a crime to murder them."

"Ella died in a terrible accident," Darius said, taking a step towards me. "The shelves collapsed. She hit her head on the pantry floor. Regrettable, but an accident. Could happen to anyone, Poppy. Even you."

I was scared but stood my ground. Benedict moved closer to me, which was nice. But there was no way I would let this terrible man frighten me. Well, not much.

"If it was an accident, why haven't the police been able to find the missing bolts from the shelves? They were fixed to the wall to avoid exactly that kind of tragedy. If they were loose and simply broke free, then the bolts would have rolled across the pantry floor. But there are no bolts. Because you unscrewed them and pocketed the bolts. Did you agree to meet her there so you could talk? Or were you hiding like a coward, waiting until she walked in so you could kill her? Either way, you planned it all out to look like an accident."

Darius stared at me, his face contorted with rage. "I am no coward. I needed Ella gone. She was a thorn in my side. I left her, but she wouldn't accept it. A man needs his freedom. He needs to be free to love whoever his heart chooses." He stopped and turned back to Florence. "And I choose you. Let's be together, Florence. Marry me."

Florence drew herself up to her full height, indignant now rather than frightened. "Absolutely not. You think I want to marry *you*? You're a few crumbs short of a biscuit!"

Darius looked horrified. "What are you talking about, my darling? We're made for each other. We're like coffee and cream. Like feta and olives ..."

Suddenly a voice boomed into the cistern. "You're like a criminal heading to jail."

"Hamish?" I said, looking upwards, where the outline of my friend was illuminated by the setting sun.

"We saw you running towards the cluster of beech trees," he replied. "So we followed you here and brought some friends with us."

Heavy boots clanged down the ladder, and DI Hembly came into view.

"Darius Bellou, I am arresting you on suspicion of the murder of Ella Cartwright. You do not have to say anything, but it may harm your defense if you do not mention when questioned something you later rely on in court. Anything you do say may be given in evidence."

He handcuffed Darius, who was too shocked to resist.

"This is a first," DI Hembly mused, walking Darius over to the ladder. "I've never arrested anyone at the bottom of a cistern before."

CHAPTER 18

"Don't think I've forgotten about you, Gerry."

I was back in my room at Broomewode Inn, packing up my things for the last time. Gerry was miserable, floating around the room with a terrific pout as if I'd lost my place in the competition to spite him. But I had a plan. After giving my statement to Sgt. Lane, I walked with the other bakers back to the inn, and on the way, I'd messaged Susan and Eve. I wouldn't leave Broomewode Village without making good on my promise to Gerry, and my coven sisters said they'd help me try to find a way to help Gerry pass over to the other side. It wasn't a full moon, but I hoped that the three of us would be able to conjure up enough magic to send Gerry on his merry way.

We arranged to meet at the magic circle at dusk. This meant I had to make my excuses (for the final time) to the other bakers, saying I'd join them in the pub for a last dinner after a little alone time. I made it seem like I needed some time to process what had happened with Darius as well as being voted off the show, but in truth, I didn't think the news had really sunk in, what with trying to save Florence from the grasp of an obsessive murderer. The events of the day would hit me later, probably when I was truly alone, soaking in the bathtub, when no one would be around if I shed a little tear or two. It had been a dramatic weekend, that was for sure. It was bound to take its toll eventually.

And so to stop Gerry's whining, I let him in on the plan. "Are you ready to experience your first magic circle?" I asked him.

"Ready for anything that gets me out of these here walls," he replied.

I didn't mention that I was worried he might not actually be able to float the distance to the forest—he seemed to be trapped between the inn and the grounds around the baking tent after all. But I figured it was best to appear confident and in control until the situation didn't allow it anymore. Ha. If only I'd been able to be that calm and collected during filming, then maybe I'd be coming back next week.

But now wasn't the time to dwell. I grabbed a warm cardi from the folded pile of clothes sitting on top of my open suitcase and gestured for Gerry to follow me downstairs.

Luckily, the other bakers were already back in the pub, no doubt about to crack open another bottle of wine, and my spirit consort and I were able to leave without being seen. Not that anyone could see Gerry, but still, walking around with him made me uneasy. I didn't want to forget myself and get caught having a chat with thin air—not when I'd made it through the last few weeks without being busted.

Enjoying the silence before Gerry would think it was safe to start jabbering on again, I let myself remember the details of the first time I attended a magic circle. It felt like a lifetime, but it was only six weeks ago. I'd never forget how kind Elspeth had been, the way she'd taken a young witch who knew nothing about her powers or her past under her wing. Elspeth's magic circle had helped me understand more about the sisterhood, but there was still a long way to go. I didn't even know if I'd managed to call the hawk for help with my spell or if he'd come all of his own accord. I just hoped that my powers were strong enough to help Gerry now.

I guided Gerry onto the narrow pebbled path lit by old-fashioned caged lanterns. Whitebeam trees flanked either side of the path like they were guarding it, and their puffy leaves swayed gently in the breeze. We walked away from the inn and the manor house on a path that grew rougher and headed into the woods. The lanterns stopped, and we had only the pale silver moonlight to guide us. I stole a look at Gerry, who had stayed unusually silent. He appeared thoughtful but determined. I was just glad that he was able to come this far from his haunting sphere.

We climbed up a hill and then took the path that crossed a patch of thick trees until we came out into the clearing where the old stones were arranged. "Whoa," Gerry said, his first words since we'd left the inn. I told Gerry the same things that Elspeth had told me the first time I visited this special place. That no one knew how or who had arranged the stones. It was a complete mystery. And then I remembered when Elspeth had warned me that sometimes we only notice the things we're already looking for. That mystic phrase of hers still rang true. I was determined to keep my eyes open going forward. Clearly I'd been blinkered by the competition, and now I had to stay open to my powers and focused on my search for my birth parents.

"The headstone is where Eve will stand as the eldest witch and lead the ceremony," I explained.

Gerry nodded. "These other stones don't look so hot."

"They're not supposed to look 'hot,' Gerry," I admonished. "They're ancient. Weathered by time and the elements. And the gaps are where stones have gone missing, moved by someone thoughtless or stolen by the local people to use for their own devices, not realizing the true value of these grand structures." I stopped. Why did Gerry always bring out the schoolmistress in me? "The local people used to take the stone and break it up to build houses and fences and things. Thankfully now things are a bit different, and the stones are protected by law."

"You're kidding me," Gerry said. "Why would the law be interested in a bunch of fossils?"

"Aren't you listening, Gerry? These stones are the very embodiment of history. All of life is contained in those rocks. They're not simply a bunch of old fossils."

"She's right," an amused voice said. "If I could see you, I'd tick you off myself."

"Susan!" I said with glee. I was so pleased to see her. "Blessed be. I've missed you this weekend. It's been … a roller coaster."

Susan hugged me. She smelled of fresh green herbs and hay. "Blessed be, Poppy. You've done very well in the competition. I hope you're suitably proud of yourself." She stood back and looked at me. "And now the next part of your journey begins."

I asked after Sly and the farm, and Susan chattered on about her happy eggs and the bees and said that Sly was his usual cheeky self—always scampering off and begging for his ball to be thrown. As she spoke, a wave of nostalgia washed over me. I already missed the farm, the animals, Susan and my other sisters.

But luckily Eve broke my musings on the past, arriving in a fluster, out of breath and apologizing for being late. "Blessed be, sisters. It wasn't easy to get away, dearies, believe me. Everyone at the inn is in shock about Darius. And Eloise, of course. Or Ella, I should say. Can't believe it myself. How could those two work in the same place and not let on? Darius walked past the wife he abandoned every single day and there was never a flicker of emotion on his face. He's a criminal as much for that as he is for her terrible murder."

Gerry cleared his throat. "Okay, Gerry, we know why we're here," I replied.

"It's quite something, watching you talk to a ghost." Eve chucked. "On the surface, you look like such a normal lass, and then BAM—ghost-whisperer."

Susan laughed, and I had to join in. It was such a relief to be myself around these women. It was the first time I'd felt relaxed all weekend.

"Anyway, we should get on," Eve said. "I've got Sol the chef covering the bar for me now we're a man down, and goodness knows if he'll be able to pull a decent pint of Guinness without my supervision."

Eve slipped a bag from her shoulder and pulled out six large church candles and three crystals, each of a different hue. She passed the reddish crystal to Susan, blue to me, and kept the green one for herself.

"Fire, water, and earth, right?" I asked.

"You're learning, dearie," Eve replied. "Very good."

The three of us maneuvered into a small circle inside the

circle of stones. I asked Gerry to step in the middle and then couldn't resist showing off my favorite new trick again to Susan and Eve. I focused on the wick of the candles and brought a spluttering flame to life.

"Bravo," Susan said.

"Let us begin," Eve said solemnly. "Gerry, we ask you to let go of all your attachments to this earth. Unshackle yourself from this temporal plane."

Gerry closed his eyes in concentration. I could see he was trying to let go—probably trying too hard, if his intense frown was anything to go by. "Soften your face," I said. "Let your shoulders relax. I've never seen such a tense ghost. You've got to let go, not hold on."

Gerry glared at me and then closed his eyes again.

Eve told us to set our crystals by our feet and join hands. I felt the familiar gentle ripple of electricity in my hand, waves reaching up into one arm and then out of the other. I had a sudden rush of compassion for Gerry, feeling for the first time the intensity of his pain being trapped. I wondered if Eve were senior enough in the coven to speak in the same ancient language that Elspeth used when she led a magic circle.

But to my surprise, Susan spoke next, calling the astral power of fire to her side. Eve gestured for me to go next, and so I copied Susan's words but calling the power of water. Eve completed the circle with earth, and then the electricity that connected our bodies turned up its frequency. I closed my eyes and let the energy take over, grateful to submit to a power larger and more mysterious than I could ever comprehend.

But I couldn't totally focus my energy on Gerry. Being at

the magic circle reminded me of my birth dad. This is where he liked to appear, full of cryptic warnings telling me to leave Broomewode Village and never come back. Despite being back in Broomewode for another weekend, I'd yet to have another message from him or my birth mom. Or unearth any new clues. Had they abandoned me again? My heart sank, and I felt miserably alone, even while surrounded by my fellow witches. At least the hawk had shown up to help me find Florence. And that majestic bird was definitely connected somehow to my dad. If only he'd show himself in human form! Last week, I'd realized that my dad appeared to me as a ghost while my mom appeared as a vision—which could mean that she was alive even if he wasn't. Part of me was hoping my dad would appear now and say something other than "you must leave." Something useful for my search for my mother if she was still alive. I needed something new to go on.

But my thoughts were interrupted by a warm feeling coming from my feet. I opened my eyes again to see that my crystal was glowing. "Whoa, cool," I whispered. But no one appeared to hear me. Eve cleared her throat and began to chant the spell.

Earth, Fire, Water, all three,
Elements of Astral, I summon thee.
By the moon's might
On this earthly night
I call to thee to give us your might.
By the power of three,
I conjure thee
To send this spirit to his resting place,

To carry his soul now full of grace.
So we will, so mote it be.
So we will, so mote it be.

Susan and I joined in for a second round, and then a third, our voices synchronizing and gaining in momentum with each new round.

Finally, Eve said, "Blessed be," and our chanting came to an end.

My eyes snapped open, eager to witness Gerry passing into a bright white light or something along those lines.

But there he was, still floating in the middle of our circle.

"Has he gone?" Susan asked.

"No!" Gerry yelped.

I repeated the answer, taking the tone down a notch. I stared at Gerry in wonder. We'd failed. He was still a ghost, still trapped on this plane. Not even the power of three witches had been able to move him on.

"Well, then, he's earthbound," Eve said, looking pretty amazed herself that our spell hadn't worked. "I've never even heard of a spirit's soul so stubborn they can resist the magic of three Broomewode witches. He'll probably go when he's ready—but not a minute before."

Gerry stomped around the circle, muttering expletives. I felt terrible. I'd tried so hard to help him pass over this time. Not for a second did I allow myself to contemplate that it might not actually work, even though I knew deep down it was a possibility. Had I given Gerry false hope? I apologized over and over again. But Gerry waved me off.

"It's okay. It's not your fault. It's me. There's something in me that's hanging on. I've got to work out what it is that's keeping me here. No more spending my days and nights goofing around, poltergeisting people. It's serious Gerry from now on. I've got to stay focused if I want to pass over. Just like you need to stay focused on the hunt for your birth parents."

Gerry was right, and I was so grateful to him for understanding and not getting mad at me. I'd thought *The Great British Baking Contest* was the pathway to finding out about my history, but although it had opened up many possible paths to the truth, I'd yet to find the right one to travel down. Now that my time was over on the show, I could put down my rolling pin and pick up my detective's hat. Someone in Broomewode Village had to know something about my mother and father, and I was going to get on the case—even if that meant investigating from afar. Now that I had a handle on names that could belong to my father, I could ask around about each man. It would take time, but now that I was out of the competition, time was my reward.

CHAPTER 19

I got a text from Florence telling me to meet everyone downstairs. They were ordering in fish and chips for dinner. This seemed like an excellent idea, as catching murderers was hungry work.

I entered the pub to a round of applause from the bakers. "Finally," said Florence. "We've been waiting to have dinner with the great Poppy Wilkinson for *ages*. You saved my life today! I want to thank you properly."

I laughed. "Sorry to keep you waiting. You should have started without me."

"Not a chance," said Gaurav. "You're the guest of honor. We even ordered extra mushy peas."

"And we've left you the seat at the head of the table," Maggie added.

The pub was still busy, but we had our usual big table, and I couldn't wait to dig into one of the newspaper-wrapped bundles. Eve brought over cutlery and plates so it felt like a proper dinner.

Florence popped another bottle of prosecco and poured for everyone.

I grinned. These guys were so nice. What was I going to do without them every weekend? I couldn't quite imagine going back to real life now. I noticed that Stanley, Florence's latest squeeze, wasn't with us. He'd probably bolted straight back to London when he realized that Florence being a man-magnet had certain drawbacks.

I took my seat at the head of table, sitting up straight like I was the queen of England. Florence to my right, then Gaurav; Hamish on my left and then Maggie. "Right, Poppy," Hamish said, addressing me firmly, "no more leaping up from the table, no more disappearing, no more Detective Wilkinson. Tonight we're here to give you a proper send-off, *Great British Baking Contest* style."

I nodded, trying to stave off the tears I could feel pricking at the edges of my eyes. Earlier, I'd told the cameras that my fellow contestants had become like family to me. But now it was time to tell them to their faces.

I raised my glass. "I want to thank all of you. I don't think I could have done it without each of you by my side. I'm sad to leave you, but I count myself very lucky that I was able to meet you."

Hamish nodded at me and smiled.

"I didn't expect to get on the show," I continued, "let alone make it to week six. I've learned so much working alongside you all. I've picked up so many tips and ideas, but the most important lesson for me has been to remember that when you bake, you bake for a reason: You're giving something to people. You're inviting them to share food, yes, but also to take part in making memories over mealtimes. A delicious cake is one thing, but it's nothing compared to sharing the stories of your day, your highs and lows, your experiences—and that's more nourishing than anything I could ever bake. So thank you for being the people who have been the real heart of this journey I've gone on these last few weeks. I'm disappointed to be leaving the show, but I'll be leaving with a full heart ..." My voice broke. "And a big bunch of new friends who feel like family to me."

I swallowed, surprised at myself for giving such an emotional speech. It was the most honest I'd been with everyone since we'd met at the beginning of filming. Not that I'd lied to anyone ... it was more that I had so many secrets I had to keep about who I really was that I always felt like I was holding something back from my friends. Otherwise, I'd end up saying things like *Now that was a particularly mean ghost* or *I'll catch up with you a sec—just saying my protection spell.*

"Och, lassie, you're bringing a tear to my eye," Hamish said.

"And mine," Maggie added. "You've reminded me why I bake in the first place: to bake with love. There's a little bit of love in everything I stir, knead, or mix. I hope it's that love that everyone can taste when they sample what I bake."

Florence leaned across the table and clasped Maggie's hands in her own. "We do," she said sincerely.

I grinned. "Now, come on, let's not get too emotional. I'm only a twenty-minute drive away. I can visit at the weekends. Let's talk about next week." I looked at their instantly sober faces and exulted for a second that I wouldn't have to worry. "It's patisserie, isn't it?"

Gaurav put his hand over his eyes. "Don't remind me. I

shall fail next week and there go my hopes of a career in baking."

We all laughed, knowing he'd never give up his career as a scientist.

I tried to relax, but there was one thing I couldn't get off my mind. Maybe Hamish could help me. I leaned next to him and lowered my voice to a whisper.

"I know we've said no more Detective Wilkinson, but I still don't understand about Edward. Why did he lie about having dinner with Eloise at his cottage? He was the police's prime suspect. It doesn't add up."

"I was confused about that, too," Hamish said. "Luckily, the old gamekeeper came to his rescue and explained everything."

"Mitty?"

"Yes. After he was released from hospital, unharmed by his ordeal, the earl rehomed Mitty at Broomewode Hall to help him recover properly from his stroke. Apparently, the chef at Broomewode Hall asked specially, and she's looking after him. They're playing a Scrabble tournament."

"Katie Donegal is looking after Mitty? That's great news, but what's this got to do with Edward?"

Hamish frowned. He didn't like it when I cut his stories short. But I needed him to get to the point! I'd jumped to conclusions about Edward, and now I was feeling guilty.

"Edward's the nice chap we always thought he was. He'd spotted that Eloise was lonely and decided to do something about it. He approached her and asked for her advice about the cottage he'd inherited in his new position as gamekeeper."

"Advice about the cottage?" I asked, confused. "How could Eloise help with that?"

"The kitchen is old, and the earl's given him a renovation budget," Hamish said. "The whole cottage is pretty run-down, to be honest, but he convinced Eloise to advise him on how to redo his kitchen."

I nodded, recalling what a state it had been in when I found Mitty locked away. It was gross, in fact, full of dirt and debris. It had obviously been neglected for years.

"I'm surprised he was so generous, to be honest, but the earl must have been feeling guilty about what had been happening right under his nose. Eloise was quick to agree, and the two of them spent a couple of evenings looking at kitchen renovation magazines together, and he cooked her dinner to say thank you. I think Eloise was awfully lonely here. Edward did her a real kindness."

I agreed with his assessment, but I was also a woman. "I'll bet she wanted Darius to see her with another man, too, hoping he'd want to reclaim her. Which didn't work."

"And may have been another reason why he killed her," Hamish said.

Oh, poor Eloise/Ella. Where Darius had been concerned, she'd been completely misguided.

"What a good-for-nothing Darius turned out to be," Hamish said. "A creep of the worst nature."

Florence butted in. "Enough shop talk, guys. I can't bear to hear that man's name." She leaned in close. "I'm not going to forget what you did for me today, Pops. You came looking for me—I know you led the search. There was a moment down there that I really thought it was the end for me. I'm swearing off men completely," she said in her dramatic way.

We all burst out laughing.

She had the grace to laugh too. "No, I'm serious. But how *did* you and Benedict manage to find us in that awful damp cistern?"

Well, Florence, I followed a magical hawk connected to my birth dad's ghost.

I smiled a little, trying not to giggle at the thought of telling her the truth. "It was Benedict's knowledge of the land that got us there in time," I replied. "He knew about its hiding places. He was invaluable really."

Florence smiled. "Well, it looks like I can thank him myself."

I followed her gaze and saw Benedict chatting with Sol the chef, who was manning the bar.

"Benedict?" Florence called.

Benedict looked round and waved. Florence gestured for him to join us.

"Oh no!" Florence gasped, clapping a hand to her mouth. "I forgot to address him by his title. Do you think I've offended him?"

I shook my head. Benedict was actually far less interested in his title and family name than I'd first thought. "Not at all," I said. "He probably enjoyed it."

Benedict walked over slowly, a pint of stout in his hand.

"Would you care to join us, sir?" Florence asked boldly. "Poppy told me that you were the one who thought to look in the cistern today, which means I owe you my life."

Florence managed to make everything sound like a line from a movie. Though I couldn't deny today had been extremely dramatic.

Benedict looked amused. He caught my eye and raised a

brow. I secretly willed him not to elaborate on our search mission. I knew that Benedict realized to some extent that I had followed the hawk's flight and had had the grace not to ask me anything about it. I was so thankful for his discretion. I didn't want to have to tell him any outright lies. Hopefully he just thought I was some kind of friendly eccentric and wouldn't think to ponder on the event any further.

Benedict cleared his throat. At over six feet tall, he towered over our table, and I had the feeling he was making the rest of the group a little nervous. He was British aristocracy, after all. "Think nothing of it. It was Poppy who acted so quickly when you disappeared earlier. It was her quick thinking that led to such a successful outcome."

Florence smiled that charming smile of hers. "Nevertheless, will you join us for a glass of bubbles? That way, I can show my gratitude and you can help us send Poppy off in style."

"It would be my pleasure. I'm glad to see you didn't suffer any ill effects from your harrowing experience."

"Not at all. In fact, think how much I can draw on this experience in my acting career."

Benedict took the seat beside Florence that she'd kept empty. I'd assumed it was for Stanley but it seemed not. "I can't believe that foolish man ever thought he had a chance with me," she said, flicking her curls over her shoulders in that coquettish way she'd mastered. So much for swearing off men. Poor Florence couldn't help herself!

Sol was helping Eve behind the bar but when there was a lull, came over. I had my mouth full of delicious crisp-battered haddock when the chef said, "Poppy, I'd love to have a quick word when you've a minute."

Oh no. My heart dropped. More bad news?

"No need to look so worried," Benedict said. "I think you might be pleased by what Sol has to say."

I turned to Sol and said, "Tell me now. Otherwise I won't enjoy my dinner wondering what you're going to say."

"Well, Eve and I had a chat earlier about what to do without Eloise, I mean Ella, sadly no longer with us." He paused. "Rest her soul. And so we thought, well, you would be perfect for the job, Poppy."

I almost choked as I swallowed my fish. "What?" I said, completely forgetting my manners in surprise. "You want *me* to be the baker for the inn?"

"Exactly," Sol replied. "We've all been following your progress on the show, and Eve speaks so highly of you that it seemed to be the most obvious fit. Our rate of pay is competitive, and we offer great training opportunities if there's a particular technique you want to learn more about. Perhaps bread might be of interest?" He chuckled.

Ouch. Too soon, Sol. But he was right. There was definitely a little room for improvement in the dough category. I laughed and looked around the table. Surely Sol wasn't being serious? But to my astonishment, everyone gave me an encouraging nod.

"Do it," Hamish urged.

"This is an amazing opportunity," Gaurav added.

"He's right," Benedict said quietly. "You'd be perfect."

Perfect. My mind lingered on the word.

I turned to Benedict. "Did you know about this?"

"I may have been consulted, but it wasn't my decision." However, he obviously hadn't said, *Poppy Willkinson? Absolutely not!* He must have given me the two lordly thumbs-up.

I'd never considered making a living from baking. Was this my true destiny? What about my graphic design business? So many thoughts flew around my head at once. Had I even missed drawing and designing while my head had been in the baking game? If I was honest with myself, then the answer was no. I'd cherished this time in the kitchen. And this way I could stay connected to Broomewode Village and the coven. I could talk to the locals more. Maybe visit Joanna in Bristol and find out what she knew about my mother's relationships.

I looked around the pub. Could this be where I came every day? Was I really that lucky?

I saw something out of the window and realized it was Gateau staring in at me. I could have sworn her little cat head nodded at me.

From the look on Benedict's face, he'd seen it too. It was a sign. I was sure of it. My familiar approved.

I stood up and offered Sol an outstretched hand, not quite believing the words I was about to say. "It would be an honor to accept the position."

Sol shook my hand, and then the whole table cheered. I glowed with pride. A new chapter of my life was beginning.

I had too many questions about my birth parents to leave Broomewode for good. Now I had an opportunity to be a local and learn more about being a water witch from my coven sisters.

Elspeth and Jonathon came in then. Elspeth swept forward when she saw me. "Did you accept the job?"

Seemed like I'd been the last one to find out. I nodded.

"What an excellent opportunity for you." She smiled her

warm, godmother smile at me. "Now we won't have to lose your company."

I was so relieved that Elspeth supported this sudden change in my life.

"Yes, well done, Poppy," Jonathon said, shaking my hand. "Now I can enjoy eating your cakes here at the inn without feeling I have to criticize them."

"And thank you for that," I said.

They headed off, and Florence, obviously still on a high from not dying, declared, "This is wonderful. Now we can turn our farewell to a celebration. Poppy's perfect for the job. And to honor how she saved my life today, I'm going to dedicate my next cake on the show to her and her new position as baker at the Broomewode Inn!"

I laughed, a warmth and sense of contentment flooding through my body. Broomewode Village was close enough that I could keep my cottage and commute if I wanted to. I couldn't believe my luck.

DINNER PASSED in a blur of good food, good friends and laughter. Benedict turned out to be a delightful dinner companion and charmed the socks off the other bakers, regaling them with stories from bygone years of Broomewode Hall, of the spectacular balls and society dramas it had once housed, the staff who had walked out after too many demanding requests from the Victorian Lady Frome. I listened, rapt, in total wonder at having that kind of connection to history, to knowing your lineage. Benedict was a fantastic storyteller, and by the end of the evening, my cheeks were sore from smiling.

But the weekend had to finally end, and as we parted ways to finish packing and load up our cars, my heart was full to bursting in the knowledge that I'd be back in a few days to begin a whole new chapter in my life.

Upstairs, Gateau was waiting for me in her favorite spot on the armchair. "Well, little one," I cooed, "you might have to give up your cozy spot, but at least you can still run free around the grounds. Sound good?"

Gateau raised her little black head and gave me a weary expression.

"That thing doesn't know when she's onto a good thing."

Gateau leapt to her feet and hissed.

"Gerry?" I said, spinning round. "How many times do I have to tell you not to float through my wall!"

Gerry grinned. "Sorry, Pops. I just wanted to come and congratulate you on the new job. I was eavesdropping downstairs while Lord Muck held court."

I told Gerry off for name-calling. Benedict wasn't half as haughty as I'd once thought. But Gerry waved away my interruption. "And obviously, I'm thrilled for me, too. I can't lie; I was very disappointed about not making it over to the other side. But now that I've got a friend here during the week, maybe being a ghost won't be so bad."

Oh yes. I hadn't figured about Gerry floating around the kitchen, telling me what I was doing wrong all week. "You have to promise not to interfere," I said firmly. "This is going to be all new to me, and I have to be able to focus. It's hard work pretending you're not there all the time."

"'Course," Gerry replied. "But I've been thinking. Maybe

this *is* the reason why I'm still here. You obviously need a guardian ghost."

Gateau meowed loudly and looked disgusted. It was her job to look after me. But maybe Gerry was onto something. If the warnings I'd received from my birth parents and the mysterious note-leaver were anything to go by, then my decision to take a job in Broomewode Village was a risky one. Not to mention my new leads about my birth dad's name. A guardian ghost might be exactly what I needed for the weeks ahead.

∾

Thank you for reading *Crumbs and Misdemeanors!* I hope you enjoyed it. Poppy's adventures in competition baking, and murder, continue in *A Cream of Passion.* Read a sneak peek below...

∾

A Cream of Passion, Chapter 1

"I'M GOING to miss having you in the tent, Poppy," Florence said. "But at least you're still here at Broomewode."

"Happily," I replied.

It was Friday afternoon, and I was back in Broomewode Village, but instead of trying to fight an onslaught of nerves ahead of a weekend of filming, I was here as a bona fide member of the community. I was a professional baker.

I'd been training with Sol, Broomewode Inn's head chef, all week, and tomorrow I'd be flying solo in my shiny new role as the inn's pastry chef. Florence had caught the train from London a day early, and we'd had lunch together at a little tea and sandwich shop after I finished my morning shift. Needless to say, with Florence around, the afternoon was about excess. We indulged in an enormous plate of finger sandwiches—soft white bread with the crusts removed and a dizzying array of fillings: egg and cress, chicken salad, cucumber and cream cheese, smoked ham and English mustard. A pretty ceramic bowl filled with salted potato chips (or crisps, as Florence kept correcting me) provided a satisfying crunch, and we drank pot after pot of steaming hot English Breakfast tea. Florence regaled me with stories of her three flatmates, all drama students and aspiring actors like her. I cracked up as she described squabbles over who was using the bathroom for too long or who had left dirty dishes in the sink again. The real drama of the week had involved two flatmates auditioning for the same role in a small theater's production of Chekhov's *Three Sisters.* "You should have heard them trying to rehearse the same lines louder than each other in their bedrooms," Florence said. "I had to turn up the radio to drown out their wailing. *I don't know why I'm so happy,*" she mimicked, placing her palm to her forehead. "*What beautiful thoughts I had, what thoughts!*"

Florence really cracked me up, and I expressed my sympathies for her plight, of course, but truthfully, I couldn't imagine sharing my little cottage with anyone. I'd been living alone for the past four years, and it was bliss. Gina, my best friend, was a short drive away and had her own set of keys to let herself in. I loved Gina to the moon and back, but would I want to live with her? No way. How could I ever share a bathroom with that girl? Hair and beauty were her trade, and she practiced what she preached. I'd never be able to shower, let alone blow-dry my hair! I'd become so accustomed to guarding myself constantly from accidentally interacting with ghosts when I was in public that I enjoyed being able to relax completely when I was home alone. Not completely alone, of course, because I had Mildred, my kitchen ghost, constantly prattling on, plus Gateau, my familiar, who had her ways of communicating, but neither of them took up counter space in the bathroom or hogged the shower.

Even when I left Mildred behind, I'd arrive in Broomewode to find Gerry, a recent and not very happy ghost waiting to show me his latest tricks.

Walking arm in arm with Florence through the village streets, I'd never felt so lucky. I had a new job, great friends in the village, and I was back on the trail to find out more about my birth parents. After Trim, a reporter for the *Broomewode News,* had put me in touch with Mavis (an inside editor at the same paper), I'd had my first proper lead about my birth mom in ages. I'd actually gone to the newspaper to find out my dad's name by scouring the old obituaries, but after having no luck, Mavis had recognized the name Valerie—she was an old school friend of her daughter, Joanna. I'd been elated, of course, and had scribbled down Joanna's details with glee. I fired off an email to her as soon as I got a moment alone. She was a solicitor, dealing with property, or so the website told me. So I wrote a short but hopefully compelling email explaining that I had some questions about a property in Broomewode Village. I figured that would be the quickest way to get Joanna's attention. I could explain more when I got her on the phone. I got a reply in seconds, but sadly it was an out-of-office. She was away on business and would be back at work Friday afternoon. Which meant I could call her as soon as Florence and I parted ways. I was beyond excited to finally speak to someone who had known my mom.

It had rained during the week, a light, refreshing drizzle, and the flowers and plants thrived from the hearty drink and were more abundant and dazzling than ever. The sun had returned from its brief vacation and was back with a vengeance, ready to outshine itself for the weekend.

"Pops, you're doing that thing again. The one where you look all dreamy and stop listening."

I apologized and told Florence that all my baking secrets were hers now that we were no longer in head-to-head competition. It was why I was steering her around the village streets in the direction of my most secret and treasured baking weapon: Broomewode Farm.

"I've always wanted to visit the farm," Florence cooed. "But you were always dashing off on some mission or another. Susan seems very charming, and I think her special friend Reginald is quite the silver fox."

Ha, trust Florence to have spotted Reg's finer qualities. Did that girl ever learn?

"Well, her eggs will blow your mind," I said, merrily skipping over the more personal comments. "She calls them her happy eggs, as her hens are so content, roaming outdoors eating organic treats. The yolks are the most perfect shade of orange you'll ever see. They make the most incredible sponge."

"Good for dessert week?" Florence said, her big eyes widening.

I'd almost forgotten that this week was dessert week on *The Great British Baking Contest*. I hadn't allowed my imagination to travel any further than each week I'd managed to get through.

"Of course!" I replied. "I can't believe we haven't discussed your recipes yet. Tell me everything."

Florence flicked her perfect chestnut curls over her shoulders and took a deep breath.

"The signature bake is cheesecake, which is my favorite dessert of all time, except for maybe sticky toffee pudding or rhubarb crumble. Oh, who am I kidding? I love *all* desserts."

She went on to excitedly tell me all about her own secret weapon—Amalfi lemons—as I continued to gently steer her along the pretty residential streets, away from the shops around the village green. It seemed like everyone who lived in Broomewode was house proud, each front garden full to the brim with flowers in bloom, lush green grass neatly trimmed. The windows gleamed, and the pastel hues of each home were as cute as candies.

Order your copy today! *A Cream of Passion* is Book 7 in the Great Witches Baking Show series.

A Note from Nancy

Dear Reader,

Thank you for reading *The Great Witches Baking Show* series. I am so grateful for all the enthusiasm this series has received. If you enjoyed Poppy's adventures, you're sure to enjoy the *Village Flower Shop,* the *Vampire Knitting Club*, and the *Vampire Book Club* series.

I hope you'll consider leaving a review and please tell your friends who like cozy mysteries and culinary adventures.

Review on Amazon, Goodreads or BookBub. It makes such a difference.

Join my newsletter for a free prequel, *Tangles and Treasons*, the exciting tale of how the gorgeous Rafe Crosyer was turned into a vampire.

I hope to see you in my private Facebook Group. It's a lot of fun. www.facebook.com/groups/NancyWarrenKnitwits

Turn the page for Poppy's special recipe for Caramelized Red Onion and Mature Cheddar Soda Bread.

Until next time,
Happy Reading,
Nancy

POPPY'S SPECIAL RECIPE FOR CARAMELIZED RED ONION AND MATURE CHEDDAR SODA BREAD

Okay, so bread is not my forte ... more like my downfall, if we're going to be honest here. But I can promise you that this recipe for soda bread is foolproof—even I managed to master this technique. If only I hadn't been so distracted on signature bake day, then maybe I might still be in the competition, but there's no time now for regrets. I've got to dust off my bread books and report for duty at Broomewode Inn next week. So I'll be practicing this larder staple a few more times in the coming days. If you caramelize the onions perfectly and make sure you're extra generous with the cheese (extra mature cheddar for good measure), then you can't go wrong. You're aiming for a sweet, buttery smell as the onions sweat down slowly—very slowly. When this part is done right, the whole bread sings with the sweetness of the onion and the gorgeous tang of melted cheese, which adds a salty depth to the loaf. I'm salivating just thinking about it.

What also makes it a winner in my eyes is that it uses the most basic of store cupboard staple items. The only drawback is that it tastes best eaten on the day it's baked. My advice is to serve the loaf still warm from the oven and slather each slice in salty, good-quality butter for an extra-indulgent kick. In the rare event you have any leftovers, then this recipe also makes for excellent toast the next day. I like to put a bit of extra cheese on mine to make a warm toastie.

Ingredients:

- 1/2 small red onion, sliced and then diced
- 50g butter (3.5 tbsp)
- 1 tbsp of rapeseed oil (Canola)
- 75g mature cheddar, grated (I cup)
- 400g self-rising flour (3 cups + 2 tsp baking powder)
- 250ml buttermilk (I cup)
- 1.5 tsp bicarbonate of soda (baking soda)

Method:

1. First up, you're going to need to get that oven preheated. You don't want that dough hanging around longer than it has to, so turn that dial to 350 degrees Fahrenheit.
2. Now heat a large frying pan over a low to medium heat and add your butter and your oil at the same time. Wait until the two ingredients have merged together (you might need to give them a swirl with a wooden spoon here).
3. Now it's time for those onions. Make sure you've diced the onion evenly, otherwise it will cook at

different times and you might end up with burnt bits (a big no-no for this bread). Fry them very slowly, stirring occasionally until they become soft, sweet and sticky. Set your pan aside to cool.

4. Next up is your flour and baking soda, which you need to mix together in a large bowl until thoroughly combined. Grate your cheese (I dare you to not nibble at a chunk) and add it to the flour bowl alongside your cooled-down onions.

5. Now slowly add your buttermilk and stir to form a dough. This is the part I find most tricky, so be careful with this step—you want your dough to feel sticky but not wet. You'll likely need the entire jug of buttermilk, but you can also judge this by hand by focusing on the texture of your dough.

6. When you're happy with the dough, turn it onto a floured surface and knead *very lightly* (seriously, guys, a light touch is everything here) until your dough is an oval or round shape. Gently place it on a baking tray or in a loaf tray/cast-iron pan, depending on what you have to hand. With a sharp knife, score the dough with a cross shape. It should go *almost* all the way through your loaf but not quite to the bottom.

7. Sprinkle with flour and send your dough into the oven with a little well-wishing prayer for 35-40 minutes. Keep a close eye on it during those last few minutes of baking—you don't want to burn the crust. You'll know your loaf is ready when the bottom feels and sounds hollow when you tap it.

8. All that's left now is to enjoy your loaf ... spread with butter or add a little extra cheese.

Bon appétit!

The Great Witches Baking Show: Culinary Cozy Mystery

Vampire Knitting Club Boxed Set: Books 7-9

Vampire Knitting Club Boxed Set: Books 10-12

Vampire Book Club: Paranormal Women's Fiction Cozy Mystery

Crossing the Lines - Prequel

The Vampire Book Club - Book 1

Chapter and Curse - Book 2

A Spelling Mistake - Book 3

A Poisonous Review - Book 4

Abigail Dixon: A 1920s Cozy Historical Mystery

In 1920s Paris everything is très chic, except murder.

Death of a Flapper - Book 1

Toni Diamond Mysteries

Toni is a successful saleswoman for Lady Bianca Cosmetics in this series of humorous cozy mysteries.

Frosted Shadow - Book 1

Ultimate Concealer - Book 2

Midnight Shimmer - Book 3

A Diamond Choker For Christmas - A Holiday Whodunnit

Toni Diamond Mysteries Boxed Set: Books 1-4

The Almost Wives Club: Contemporary Romantic Comedy

An enchanted wedding dress is a matchmaker in this series of romantic comedies where five runaway brides find out who the best men really are!

Take a Chance: Contemporary Romance

Meet the Chance family, a cobbled together family of eleven kids who are all grown up and finding their ways in life and love.

For a complete list of books, check out Nancy's website at NancyWarrenAuthor.com

ABOUT THE AUTHOR

Nancy Warren is the USA Today Bestselling author of more than 100 novels. She's originally from Vancouver, Canada, though she tends to wander and has lived in England, Italy and California at various times. While living in Oxford she dreamed up The Vampire Knitting Club. Favorite moments include being the answer to a crossword puzzle clue in Canada's National Post newspaper, being featured on the front page of the New York Times when her book Speed Dating launched Harlequin's NASCAR series, and being nominated three times for Romance Writers of America's RITA award. She has an MA in Creative Writing from Bath Spa University. She's an avid hiker, loves chocolate and most of all, loves to hear from readers!

The best way to stay in touch is to sign up for Nancy's newsletter at NancyWarrenAuthor.com or www.facebook.com/groups/NancyWarrenKnitwits

To learn more about Nancy and her books
NancyWarrenAuthor.com